THE FROZEN CEILING

Rona Randall

When Tessa Pickard found the note amongst her father's possessions, instinct told her that THIS had been responsible for his suicide, not the professional disgrace which had ruined his career as a mountaineer and instructor. The note was cryptic, anonymous, and bore a Norwegian postmark. Tessa promptly set out for Norway, determined to trace the anonymous letter-writer, but unprepared for the drama she was to uncover — or that compelling Max Hyerdal, whom she met on board a Norwegian ship, was to change her whole life.

D0837423

GHOSTMAN

Kenneth Royce

Jones boasted that he never forgot a face. When he was found dead outside the National Gallery it was assumed he had remembered one too many. The man he had claimed to have identified had been publicly executed in Moscow some years before. The presumed look-alike was called Mirek and his background stood up. The Security Service calls in Willie 'Glasshouse' Jackson — Jacko — as they realise that there is a more sinister aspect. Jacko and his assistant begin to unearth commercial and political corruption in which life is cheap and profits vast, as the killing machines swing into action.

John D. MacDonald was born in Sharon, Pennsylvania. A graduate of Syracuse University and Harvard School of Business Administration, he began his writing career when he was serving overseas with the United States Army during World War II. Instead of the usual letter home, he wrote a story to his wife, Dorothy, which she successfully sold to a magazine. His move into 'pulps' meant that his first novel was published in America in 1950. This led on to over seventy books written in his lifetime, as he became one of the most widely read thriller writers in the world. His success was particularly recognized for his *Travis McGee* series, leading to critical acclaim and prestigious awards.

John D. MacDonald died on Christmas Day 1986.

JUDGE ME NOT

Teed Morrow is home from Europe and the post-war challenge of giving people back 'a measure of trust and faith and hope'. He wants a break from getting involved. But the old evils of corruption and cruelty are there waiting for him in his new job. Some ruthless people are not going to let him, or anyone, spoil things for the city hall 'fat cats' and their friends. Suddenly, he needs an alibi for a murder — those he loves are in serious danger — and all he values begins to fall rapidly apart.

Books by John D. MacDonald
Published by The House of Ulverscroft:

A DEADLY SHADE OF GOLD

JOHN D. MacDONALD

$\blacklozenge$

JUDGE ME NOT

Complete and Unabridged

ULVERSCROFT
Leicester

First published in Great Britain in 1999 by
Robert Hale Limited
London

First Large Print Edition
published 2001
by arrangement with
Robert Hale Limited
London

The moral right of the author has been asserted

All characters in this book are fictional and any
resemblance to persons living or dead
is purely coincidental.

British Library CIP Data

MacDonald, John D. (John Dann), *1916 – 1986*
Judge me not.—Large print ed.—
Ulverscroft large print series: adventure & suspense
1. Suspense fiction
2. Large type books
I. Title
813.5′4 [F]

ISBN 0–7089–4406–X

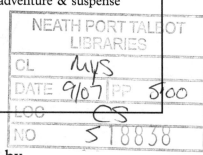
Published by
F. A. Thorpe (Publishing)
Anstey, Leicestershire

Set by Words & Graphics Ltd.
Anstey, Leicestershire
Printed and bound in Great Britain by
T. J. International Ltd., Padstow, Cornwall

This book is printed on acid-free paper

1

When the woman left his side he turned, in his sleep, toward the window.

The late October sun slanted across West Canada Lake, rebounded from the locked shutters of the other camps, shone with faint warmth through the open window of Teed Morrow's rented camp, shone red through his closed eyelids as he let himself drift slowly up from a nap of pure relaxation. He lay naked on the red and blue Indian blanket, a rangy, deep-chested man, with muscles laced tightly to the angular bones. The brown hair on his arms and legs was bleached lighter than his summer tan. He yawned and sat up slowly, stretching his left arm until the shoulder popped, scratching his chest with the knuckles of his right hand. His features were heavy, and his eyes were chronically sleepy, and his hair was a tight cap of brown-blond wire, thinning just a bit on top.

He squinted appreciatively across the lake at the fading fire-colors of autumn on the slopes of the Adirondack hills, and felt sad that this was nearly the last of the week ends before the camp was taken over by winter.

1

The distant hiss of the shower stopped and the water pump chugged on for a few minutes before it stopped too. He flipped a mental coin and decided on a swim. His trunks were still beside the bed where he had dropped them. As he stood up to pull them on he noticed how neatly the mayor's wife had arranged her clothes on the cane-bottomed chair at the foot of the bed. Nubby fall suit, with coat fitted over the back of the chair, skirt folded neatly. High-heeled alligator pumps standing side by side, an inch from the hanging toes of the empty nylons.

A very neat woman. Very careful. Very calmly and carefully sensuous, a quality making this little affair quite safe while at the same time robbing it of the spice which recklessness would have sharpened.

The door of the tiny bathroom swung open and she came out with her faintly, intriguingly knock-kneed walk. She had her head lowered so that the dark hair, damp from the shower, had fallen forward over one eye. She was biting her underlip and her arms were craned up behind her, fastening the bra. Her breasts were small, her hips tautly narrow, the sheer whiteness of the bra and panties startling against the almost mahogany tan.

'There,' she said. She tossed her head, flinging the dark hair back, standing smiling at him with measured warmth, with only a trace of consciousness of self.

He knew that her pride was in her girl's body, in her unsagging tautness, in nut brownness that the years — she would not tell him how many, though he guessed thirty-four — had not touched, and so he always felt a strong obligation to make a small salute in the general direction of that pride.

He shook his head, clucking. 'Not over seventeen, miss.'

'Great fool! What woke you up? I was going to sneak out.'

'Sun in my eyes. And you floundering and splashing around in there.'

She picked up shoes and nylons and sat on the edge of the bed. She pulled the stockings on, her face intent on this small task, and he stood and watched her, trying to gauge within himself the extent of renewed desire, because this was the measure of how long this thing would last. And, instead of desire, he saw a meagerness about her body. In her face there was a touch of something simian.

Felice slipped the pumps on, stood up and walked away from the bed and looked down and backward around her hips, curving her shoulder out of the way. 'Seams straight, Teed?'

'Straight. Say, how about your hair?'

'You mean wet? I'll leave the top down. It'll be dry by the time I get back to Deron.'

She took her purse off the high bureau, turned and smiled at him. 'If you're going to kiss me, better do it before I get my face on.'

He tilted her chin up, kissed her lightly, quickly.

'And is that all?' she pouted.

'For the nonce, Mrs Carboy.'

He sat on the bed and watched her apply the careful make-up, then don blouse, skirt, tailored jacket. She had brushed her hair into shape. The last thing she did was take a pair of tinted glasses with heavy dark frames and put them on. It was the last touch which always seemed to turn her into a reasonably prosperous librarian. She looked at her watch. 'Lots of time.'

She sat beside him on the bed. He took her purse, dug out two cigarettes, handed her one. She detested having her cigarettes lit for her then handed to her.

He struck the match. He lit hers and then, as he was lighting his own, she said, 'What do you think of me, Teed?'

'I think you're the poor man's chameleon. Twenty minutes after you leap out of bed, you look ready to be speaker at the luncheon club. Unflattering, I call it.'

'Teed! I don't mean that way. I mean when

4

you met me.' She swung a crossed leg and pouted.

'Let me see. That was in hizzoner's office. There I was, a clean young civil servant, looking lustfully at the mayor's wife.'

'Be serious, Teed.'

'OK, so I saw a gleam in your eye.'

'Other men haven't seen it.'

'Oh, I'm always alert for a gleam like that. And frankly, hizzoner didn't strike me as the sort of old party who could do very much about that gleam.'

She gave him a cool look. 'So the perceptive Teed Morrow decided then and there that I was a loose woman. Now who's unflattering?'

'No. Not then and there. That was just a preliminary survey. I rechecked it that night I bummed a ride home with you after the late work.'

'Rechecked!' she said scornfully. 'Masterful type, aren't you? The subtle approach. Fat chance I had to say yes, no, or maybe.'

'People say no to hesitant people just because they think they should.'

She looked down and drew crosses on the back of his hand with a pointed fingernail. From his angle of vision he could look into the curve of her throat, see the slow beat of a visible pulse.

'What's the matter with me, Teed?' she asked softly. 'I ought to feel rotten, all the way through. And my conscience doesn't hurt a bit. I just don't want to be caught, and that's all I care.'

'What are you working up to, Felice?'

She lifted her eyes slowly to his. Her lips were not far from his. Her mouth trembled, and he felt almost certain that she had made it tremble.

'Would I be too terribly silly if I sort of . . . kid myself, Teed?'

'In what way?'

'Well . . . thinking that doing this with you might help Mark.'

He stared at her and wanted to laugh. 'Now wait a minute, Felice! Let's get back on where I fell off. Item — Mark Carboy is the mayor, and your husband. Item — Mark Carboy is a slightly stupid man, a figurehead for the Raval mob. Item — my boss, Powell Dennison, is the new city manager who is very frankly out to take the city away from Raval. What am I supposed to do? Go up to Powell and say, 'Please, Mr Dennison, you got to take it easy on Carboy because I'm sleeping with Mrs Carboy'?'

She winced. 'Damn you, do you have to say it that way?'

'Then tell me what you mean.'

She shrugged. 'Everybody calls you Denni-son's hatchet man, ever since he sent for you six months ago. If you wanted to help Mark, you could find a way.'

'If I wanted to.'

She looked down again and ran her fingertips up the back of his wrist. 'Do you want to take my silly little rationalisation away from me, darling?'

'And if I did?'

'I just really don't see how I could . . . let myself go on with this. I mean I love you and need you so dreadfully and all that, but . . . '

'You'd like to think you were really doing it for Mark, eh?'

She didn't look up. 'Don't be cruel to me, Teed.'

'I suppose you want me to promise.'

'Oh, yes, Teed. Just a little promise. And it won't hurt anybody. Mark isn't dangerous.' He saw her mouth twist. 'He's just a fool.'

He felt remote, apart from the two figures sitting on the bed, almost as though he were a third person — judicious, objective, slightly scornful. No matter how soulfully they could manage to look at each other, no matter how suggestively her fingertips nibbled at his arm, it was still a tired little scene that did neither of them any particular credit. He wondered if his sudden desire to humiliate her arose simply from a feeling of revulsion at this trade she wanted to make.

'That's something I ought to think over.'

She gave him a wide-eyed stare. 'Think? For heaven's sake, why?'

'I should promise, eh? Like that. Because you ask me to.'

'No. Because I mean something to you, Teed.'

'Sure you do, kitten. You mean a lot to me.'

She took off the heavy-rimmed glasses, leaned back, bracing herself with her arms, looking at him with a shy, inviting smile.

'It isn't really as late as I thought, Teed,' she said. 'Tell me what I mean to you.'

'A near miss, Felice.'

She stiffened. 'What does that mean?'

'All along it's been a good try. But your love-making, my sweet, has been under very precise control. Your little frenzies have been so very exact. Like you have an outline in the back of your mind, a sort of picture of Felice enjoying herself, and you follow it right down to the last semicolon.'

For a few moments her face was utterly expressionless. He felt as though he could actually hear the tiny click as the decision dropped into place in her mind. She pivoted suddenly, kicking her feet up, falling back across his lap, looking up at him.

'Of course it was that way, Teed,' she said. 'But now it will be better. I didn't realize I had that . . . reserve. Now you've explained it to me. Now that I know you'll help silly old Mark, the . . . last barriers can drop, Teed. The very last. I'll be the most perfectly wanton thing. Hold me, Teed. Hold me tight. Maybe now I can really completely forget myself. Please, Teed.'

No, baby, he thought. You've never forgotten yourself and you never will. You are a trim, tight, controlled little package, and in your little blindnesses and incoherences, your little love-cries, you've been reading your lines off a script in the back of your mind. I've heard the pages rattle as you turned them.

He let her wait. He made no move. Something quite close to hate stirred behind her eyes, even as she was making them heavy-lidded. He could sense her surprise that he did not plead for a continuance of this timetabled, double-spaced, rigorously out-lined affair in which each posturing, each body juxtaposition had been as curiously impersonal as the complex figures of an ancient dance with stern rules and forgotten significances. Her little excitements had been doled out by the cc., and her rapt functions had been performed with the practised

9

economy and elegance of the expert.

He was a little surprised at the relief he felt that it was now over, as though the shame had come, not from the necessary subterfuges of adultery, but from a sense of misdirected functioning, as though he were an adolescent now giving up forbidden solitary experiments.

So he shook his head sadly and said, 'All for Mark, eh? My lamb, the merchandise is attractive, but the markup is too high.'

He caught her wrist when her curved nails were inches from his eyes. She tore herself free. He sat placidly and watched her pace in restless anger.

'A truly astonishing vocabulary,' he said mildly.

She suddenly fought for control, achieved it quickly. 'All right, Teed. I'll mark it up as a waste of effort.' She gave her flashing simian grin, and he liked her for it. 'An enjoyable waste, but a waste.'

'I could ease the blow a little for Mark, but what's the point? He's in deep. People generally pay for their deeds.'

'Aren't you a little righteous, Teed?'

'That business about pots and kettles isn't written into the statutes yet. We are going to have to see each other around town, Felice. Let's not end it on too bad a note. Would it look too silly if we shook hands?'

'Like the old joke about the monkeys? It would be silly, but there's no one here but us chickens.' She walked over to him as he stood up. He had always liked her walk. A taut, brisk little walk, feet coming down firmly. It called attention to the cleverness of assembly of the joints and tendons of ankle, knee, and hip. He handed her the glasses and she put them on, put on at the same time the little earnestness that went with the glasses, a social-worker, Wellesley-graduate, only-the-best-books earnestness.

She shook hands a bit uncertainly, like an actress who discovers that the last sheet of her radio script is unaccountably missing.

There was nothing to gather up, for in all previous visits to the camp she had left nothing. She took her purse and they walked out to the slightly shabby convertible which was the second car of the honourable Carboy family.

'I shall never forget you, Teed,' she said seriously.

'Take it easy on the way back. The roads are tricky at dusk, Felice.'

'You won't ever . . . oh, hint or anything to anybody?'

For one moment her mask of precision and calmness slipped, and there was something naked and afraid in her eyes. She sat behind the wheel, jacket unbuttoned. And looking at her, he knew how he had missed in the beginning, how he had never thought of the very obvious device of extreme roughness, of hands careless of the softness of her. And in the moment of ending all of it, he knew it was possible to begin it again, and on a different and better basis.

So he patted her shoulder very lightly and said, 'Take care, honey,' then stood and watched the car bounce on the ruts of the short lane, turn sharply onto the highway. The motor drone faded away down the two-lane asphalt that half circled the lake.

Teed wandered back into the camp, oddly restless. There was little left of her. A towel, still steamy, on the shower rail. Four cigarette butts, red-smeared, in the flat brass tray. Two long black hairs caught in his brush. An indentation in the pillow where she had napped. He hung the towel out on the line, emptied the ash tray into the chunk stove, fluffed out the pillow. He pulled the hairs from the white bristles of the brush and, remembering a childhood trick, held them tightly as he ran thumb and fingernail down the length of them. They sprang into black, tight-coiled springs, and that was supposed to mean that you were healthy.

★ ★ ★

The last of the sun was gone when he walked down to the dock. He went off in a flat drive, came up snorting, lifting his arms in a slow powerful crawl. A hundred yards offshore he rolled onto his back and floated, thought about Felice. She probably loved Mark Carboy, the fumbling old fool. Felice was a second wife. The children of the first marriage were grown, living far away.

There was prestige in being the wife of the mayor. Even, under the brand-new City Manager Plan, a figurehead mayor. But Felice hadn't saved him, couldn't save him.

Teed Morrow felt a hard excitement as he thought of how he and Powell Dennison were going to break the city of Deron wide open.

Powell Dennison had been his faculty advisor when Teed had majored in political science. There had been mutual respect, friendship. Then during the occupation years, Colonel Dennison had wangled a transfer of Captain Morrow to his AMG command in Germany. Together they had broken the hold of the ex-Nazis, given the people a measure of trust and faith and hope, set up a town that later became a model for all military government in the western zone.

And after five years of infrequent correspondence, Powell Dennison had sent for him again, brought him to upstate New York from a job as director of a taxpayers' research bureau in western Pennsylvania, crammed his appointment as Assistant to the City Manager down the throats of the Common Council.

'This,' said Powell Dennison, 'is going to be a toughy. That's the way you like them, Teed, isn't it?'

'With minor reservations.'

'Two hundred thousand people here. A slick little bastard named Raval has been city boss since before he was old enough to vote. Not only does he wax fat on the horse-room take, whorehouse row, kickbacks from cops and firemen, punchboards, slots, dope . . . in fact, the whole usual line of racketeer arrangements, but he owns the city government, lock, stock, and barrel. His companies bid against each other for the privilege of paving the streets, building the schools, digging the sewers. On the surface it looks like a two-party system, but actually nobody gets into office who isn't willing to play ball with Lonnie Raval. His goons control the wards which swing the balance of power one way or the other. There was a big yen for reform last year among the better citizens. So Lonnie threw them a bone. He let this City

Manager thing go through. He figured he could handle anybody who landed on the hot spot. That means me. I am going to be a serious surprise to Mr Lonnie Raval.'

'Sounds like fun.'

'More than that, Teed. It's dangerous. Lonnie Raval is tied in with the eastern syndicate. He can import his hard boys when he needs them. The dope setup ties him in with the Mafia, and you know what playmates they can be. If we take a bang at things as soon as we uncover them, he'll pull our cork. So we work hard, do a lot of digging, and explode things all at once.

'Some local businessmen who don't want their names to enter into this thing have put up a secret fund. It's substantial. And cheaper for them in the long run if we can swing it.'

★　★　★

He shivered suddenly, rolled over, and headed back for the dock. It had been a rough and exciting six months. The affidavits were beginning to pile up in the safe-deposit box. Enough had leaked out so that a lot of people were nervous. Felice had been nervous, and with cause. Mark Carboy's name appeared on some of those affidavits. Powell Dennison hadn't set the date for dropping the whole mess in the District Attorney's lap, with copies to one of the two daily papers with enough guts to spread the slime all over the front page. Teed hoped it would be soon. The tension and suspense were beginning to be a bit wearing.

Once he had showered and towelled himself dry, he wondered whether he'd stay or head back for the city. It was Sunday night. He padded into the kitchen and inspected the larder. Couple of cans of soup, one of beans, one of spaghetti. Sunday, October what? Last Sunday was the twenty-first. That would make it . . .

He grinned and snapped his fingers. His grin was a bit shamefaced. Today was his birthday and it was the first time he had thought of it. Thirty-one today. Oddly, it made the larder look most inadequate. A man owes himself a steak on his birthday.

Once upon a time birthdays had been part and piece of the long warm years of childhood. A dollar in an envelope from Aunt Marian. The BB rifle you weren't sure you'd get. The deep insuck of air and the hope that every candle would go out. Every last one. And a birthday made a difference in the world, in the whole world.

And then a birthday becomes like a milepost that you see from a train window,

16

and if you forget to look at the proper moment, it is gone. And nobody in the wide world gives a damn whether you happen to notice that milepost or not, so celebrating is like the whistling you do on a narrow lane at night where the trees meet overhead, forming a fearful tunnel. You have buried your people, and your kid sister was in that WAC queue outside the London theatre when the V-1 found them. And the lovely Ronnie who was everything to you, married a dark trim little man who is doing quite well in the insurance business out in Dayton, and the last Christmas card, forwarded three times, was a heartbreaking cartoon of the lovely Ronnie and the dark man and the toddler and the baby and the two dogs.

But a man owes himself a steak and a few drinks and, afterward, a pleasant muzziness wherein he can sit and smoke with slower gestures than usual and think long pseudo-philosophic thoughts of time and life and how very dead you will eventually be when at last there are no mileposts and no window to see them from and no train clattering endlessly on.

Since it was his birthday, Teed Morrow dressed with special care. French linen shirt, the Shetland jacket, tawny gabardine slacks. He locked the camp, and the faint starlight

17

made metallic glints on the gleaming black of the Ford convertible. White headlights cut a shocking hole in the night, and leaving the top up, he drove without haste toward Deron, the radio barely audible, and he told himself that he was not the least bit lonely. He told himself one time too many, and became sourly amused. Spectacle of a man kidding himself.

2

For the sake of privacy, he had moved from the Hotel Deron during his second month in the city, had found a so-called garden apartment on the north edge of town, a new development on Bannock Road just off the main east-west highway. The red brick units contained four apartments apiece, each with its private entrance. The units were so placed that each apartment looked out on a reasonable amount of open space and greenery rather than onto other windows.

Had he been living entirely on the rather meagre salary Dennison had been able to swing for him, the apartment would not have been possible. But, in a period of conservatism following his father's death, he had tied up the rather substantial inheritance so that he could not touch the principal. It brought in approximately two thousand dollars a year, and this made the difference between living carefully and living with a certain style.

The development had the advantage of having a central switchboard and messenger service, as well as maid service for those who wanted it. He pulled in by the office and went inside. Mrs Kidder, the slim, shy, overworked wife of the manager, was at the switchboard, behind the high counter.

'Mr Dennison called you three times this afternoon, Mr Morrow. The last time he left the message you should come out to his house if you got back before ten.'

Teed frowned and looked at his watch. A little after eight. He smiled at Amy Kidder. 'Thanks, honey.'

She blushed. 'Now, Mr Morrow!'

'As long as your husband doesn't catch on, we're safe, aren't we?'

It was an old game between them, one that he knew delighted her, and never failed to make her blush. He winked solemnly at her, and went out and got in the car. There was annoyance at having to run out to Powell Dennison's house just because the man happened to whistle for him, but the thought that it might be something hot, something new, muffled the annoyance.

Powell Dennison had rented a large, ugly frame house in one of the older sections of Deron. It was zoned residential, yet surrounded by areas that had been rezoned commercial. Teed parked in the narrow driveway.

As he went up the last step onto the porch, the front door opened, silhouetting Powell against the hall light.

'Glad you decided to come back to town, Teed. Come on in.' The voice, like the man, was slow, warm, sincere. He was a big man in his early fifties. Hard fat had larded the athlete's body. In the firm, florid flesh of his face, the gray eyes were level, honest, and unafraid. This man, Teed knew, had a mind so quick and so certain that, as an administrator, he could have scratched high on the tree in either private industry or state or federal government. Yet his passion was city government, his skill the rejuvenation of weary cities, his creed the potential grass-roots impact of awakened citizens. It was not his fault that he lived in an era when such dedication was poorly paid. Teed had long since decided that Powell would have continued with his work, somehow, even if it were without any salary at all.

Powell led Teed into the high narrow living room with its ugly rented furniture, brown floral wallpaper, shallow unusable fireplace. Marcia Dennison, the elder of the two daughters, sat in an overstuffed chair, one leg pulled up under her, a book in her lap. She was twenty-three. She did the marketing, and the cooking, in addition to working five mornings a week in a local secretarial school, teaching typing classes. Though it would have

21

been extremely simple for Powell Dennison to have found part-time work for her with the city government, it was the sort of thing that he would never do.

Though she had never indicated as much, Teed had the strong feeling that Marcia disliked him. She was a lithe blonde, firm-lipped, with her father's grey eyes, with his air of calmness. Wherever she sat, however she stood, she seemed to be carefully posed, as though awaiting the pop of flashbulbs, yet he knew she was not vain. He always thought that the women of the Vikings had probably been like Marcia. Lithe grace concealed the essential sturdiness of thighs, the lioness loins. She sat there, in a cashmere cardigan that was not quite right for her because the shade of yellow took lustre from her hair.

Jake, the other daughter, the dark, flashing, eighteen-year-old, the one most adored by Powell because she was like the wife who was now dead, was another matter. Entirely another matter, with her gawky ripeness, wide-lipped breathlessness, and hero-worshipping mind which had not yet caught up to bright lushness of the woman-body. She had been reading a paper spread on the floor and as Teed came in, she bounded up, came swinging toward him in jeans and T shirt, eyes bright with the ever embarrassing worship, lips smiling for him, dark hair rumpled, smoothing it now with the back of her hand, with a woman-gesture not quite right for the child mind.

She caught his arm. 'Oh, Teed. Teed, it's your birthday!'

Jake hugged his arm, cheek against his shoulder, round breast-firmness all too evident in its pressure against his upper arm. It was good to know that someone else had remembered.

'And there's a cake,' she said.

Marcia smiled faintly. 'Under pressure. I said you wouldn't want one.'

He met Marcia's level glance. 'But I do. And thank you.'

'I would have made it, Teed,' Jake said, 'but my cakes are godawful.' She let go of his arm and made a face, comically forlorn.

'You can have him back in a few minutes, girls,' Powell said. 'Come on into the study, Teed. I've got something to show you.'

Teed had suspected for a long time that Powell had hopes of his one day marrying Marcia. Teed knew that Powell had no illusions about him, about his private life, and he guessed that Powell reasoned that, after marriage, Teed would settle down. Maybe Marcia's coolness was the result of having guessed what her father dreamed.

Powell Dennison shut the door of the small study and pointed to a box on the table. 'Have a cigar, Teed.'

'Never use them. Thought you knew that, Powell.'

Powell gave him an enigmatic smile. 'Take a look at the contents.'

Teed looked at the open cigar box. One cigar was missing, and through the gap where it had been, he could see the green gleam of currency. He picked some more cigars out of the top row.

'Don't bother,' Powell said. 'I counted it all and replaced it. Five thousand in cash. I went down this morning to get in a little work. It was on my desk, wrapped in brown paper. My name printed on it in pencil.'

Teed grinned at him. 'We've got them worried.'

'It looks crude, but it's pretty smooth, Teed. No proof. No receipts. No demands. I'm supposed to quietly pocket the dough. That puts me very gently on the hook.'

Teed ran his thumb along the edge of the box. 'It will be a pleasure to take them back.'

'I thought you might enjoy it, Teed.'

'I'll go out in the morning.'

'Fine,' said Powell in the tone that meant the subject was closed. He opened his desk drawer, took out a small package, gaily wrapped. 'From the Dennisons,' he said gruffly.

'Now, Powell. You didn't have to . . . '

'Have to? Listen to the man. Come on out where the girls can see you open it. Had your dinner?'

'Not yet.'

'Marcia'll fix that. And I'll fix a shaker of stingers — a personal shaker for you, Teed.'

Because the dining room was more than grim, the Dennisons had a snack and Teed had a pickup dinner in the big light kitchen, the present, still wrapped, by his plate. Jake shouted from the next room and Marcia turned off the lights. Jake came in bearing the cake, the light of the candles shining on her smiling lips, dark glint of eyes. They sang in the traditional way and Teed gathered in his breath and whoofed at the thirty-one candles, seemingly getting them all until, when he had no breath left, one of them flicked back into pallid life. Marcia walked to the light switch again and they blinked at the sudden brightness. He opened the package. It was a silver lighter, a good one. He took the old battered one from his pocket, leaned forward in the chair, and flipped it into the metal wastebasket beside the sink.

Marcia came to him where he sat and put a hand lightly on his shoulder and leaned over to kiss him lightly. 'Happy birthday, Teed,' she said. Her lips were cool and soft.

Jake had walked over to the other side of him. 'Happy birthday, Teed,' she said, and her voice was shaky and something had gone wrong with her eyes. Her arm went strong around his neck and her lips came down on his, lips that felt swollen and seemed to pulse against his mouth. He knew at once that this kiss was wrong, that this kiss would spoil the mood so carefully constructed. He knew that he should force it to end without being too obvious about it, and her lips had parted against his and already the kiss had lasted too long, had become too intense.

He forced her away gently, heard Marcia's nervous laugh. Jake stood and looked down at him, with that wrongness still in her eyes.

'Better put it to bed, Jake,' Powell said, with too much joviality in his tone. Marcia's eyes were watchful.

'Yes,' Jake said, never taking her eyes from Teed's, 'there's school tomorrow, isn't there? And there's a hell of a lot of candles on that cake, isn't there?'

'Jake!' Powell said sharply.

She walked with too much casualness, too much hipsway, to the kitchen door, standing for a moment, looking at them, posing in a way that was comic drama and pathos at the same time. 'Good night, all,' she said, looking only at Teed.

They were silent until the stair creak had ended, until her bedroom door had banged shut.

Powell sighed. 'A handful, that one.'

Marcia put her elbows on the table, rested her chin on her fist. 'She thinks she's in love with you, Teed. Been mooning around lately. She's never been — quite this obvious about it before.'

It was a relief to have it in the open. 'It puts me on a spot,' he said.

'I know,' Marcia said.

'What spot? What kind of spot?' Powell demanded.

'Don't you see it, Daddy?' Marcia said, almost impatiently. 'If he laughs at her or brushes her off too hard, she'll do something terribly silly, or terribly wrong. If he acts so that she thinks he's encouraging her, it will just get worse. Teed has to walk right on top of the fence until she gets over it.'

Teed gave her a grateful look.

'By next summer,' Powell said, 'she'll be working at that summer camp, and then in September she'll be going away to school.'

'October to June seems short to you, Daddy. To Jake it's like several years.'

'I'll have a talk with her,' Powell said heavily.

'Please,' Marcia said. 'No.'

Later, after the dishes were cleaned up, Powell Dennison made one of his customary awkward attempts to throw Marcia and Teed together. 'You see him out, please, Marcia. Teed, let me know as soon as you get back in the morning.'

Teed and Marcia went out onto the front porch. The midnight was cool. She leaned against the railing, her arms folded against the cold. He stood with the cigar box, rewrapped in the brown paper, under his arm.

'I think you're handling it very well,' Marcia said.

'Oh, Jake? I'm not doing anything. She's quite a kid, you know.'

'She's a very lusty young girl,' Marcia said remotely. The distant street light touched her pale hair, making it look silver, making it look like the smooth sheen of fast water in moonlight.

' 'Night, Marcia. Thanks for the party.'

'Good night, Teed.'

As he backed out the driveway he saw that she still stood there, hips braced against the railing, arms folded, shoulders slightly hunched. In some obscure way she always managed to annoy him. She was like the clear ice on a winter stream where, if you look closely, you can imagine that you see the water bubbling by underneath. Seven years of responsibility for the household. Maybe that had done it.

Responsibility like that could do odd things to a girl like Marcia. With the death of her mother, the home could have fallen apart. Powell Dennison, with his dedication to his work, Jake, with her streak of wildness, both needed some focal point, some sane stability on which to depend. Marcia gave of herself, gave up her freedom, gave up a part of her individuality, for the sake of the home.

And, as with all forms of martyrdom, Teed knew that the danger was that she would learn to like it, possibly had already begun to like it, to value the deep sad wells of self-pity more than the lost freedom.

Once again he found himself thinking of the lovely Ronnie, of days long gone. Ronnie, who couldn't wait. Ronnie, the Dayton wife of the insurance man. He knew he had been a fool to expect her to wait. There was no waiting in Ronnie. A war made no difference to her vast insatiable impatience.

So the little dark man had grabbed her deftly a month after Teed had left. There had been two possible futures for Ronnie. Either someone married her and chained her with children, with clockwork pregnancies, or she would become a tramp — not because there was any evil in her, any coarseness — but merely because she was driven and harried and spurred on by both a strong consciousness of the passing of time, and by the delusion that there was only one way, one fundamental way of making time stand still for a little while. Teed knew the accepted explanations of nymphomania. None of them seemed to fit Ronnie. He had a symbolic picture of her in his mind. A tiny naked Ronnie running, endlessly screaming, down a narrow empty street, running by all the sleep-shops, by the window displays of bedroom suites, by the deodorant and cosmetic ads that implored her to smell better, taste better, look juicier, acquire that wanted look — while behind Ronnie bounded the tireless beast which has a clock dial instead of a face, and carries the little packages of wrinkles, of gray hairs, of varicose veins, of sagging wattled tissues. In a nation where youth is a synonym of happiness, time-conscious women spend billions to cheat the hand of a clock, to prove that a calendar can lie. Teed went to sleep while playing the frayed old game entitled What Might Have Been. And Ronnie walked into his dreams, carrying a little wooden purse shaped exactly like a coffin, and one of the silver handles was actually a lipstick.

★　★　★

At nine-thirty the next morning Teed turned into the drive of Lonnie Raval's home on Roman Hill, in one of the most exclusive residential suburbs of Deron. The drive slanted up to an oval turn-around with a three-car garage beyond it, an antique lamppost on a patch of green in the middle of it.

A small, stringy, dish-faced man wearing a white jacket came out the side door and stood waiting for Teed to approach.

'I'd like to see Mr Raval.'

'Out in the back. What's in the box?'

'Cigars. I'm . . . '

'I know who you are, Morrow, and where you work. He's out in the back.'

Teed walked around the garages. He glanced back. White-jacket was following him at a careful thirty-foot interval. Lonnie Raval stood forty feet behind the garage. New golf balls were blazing white against the grass. Lonnie had an iron in his hand. He was a tanned man of medium height with strong shoulders. He was dark-haired, entirely

31

unremarkable except for his eyes, which were long-lashed, liquid, melting black.

He smiled at Teed. 'Hi, fella! Glad to see you. OK, Sam.' White-jacket turned without a word and went back around the garage toward the house.

'Trying to get more loft and more backspin,' Lonnie explained. He addressed a ball, swung hard. The ball went out in an arc that was too flat. A hundred yards down the manicured slope, a leggy brunette in a chartreuse sun-suit scuffed over to the ball, picked it up and put it into the cloth bag she carried. There was something bored and petulant about her stance and her walk.

'Now what the hell am I doing wrong, Morrow?'

Teed moved over behind him. 'Try it again, Mr Raval.'

'How many times I got to tell you to call me Lonnie, fella?' He prodded another ball out of the group, addressed it, swung. The result was the same.

The girl picked it up. 'I'm gettin' tired, Lonnie,' she called, her voice coming thinly up the slope.

'Just keep picking up the balls, you,' Lonnie shouted back. Teed saw her shrug.

'Try placing the ball more off your right foot,' Teed said. 'You're trying to scoop them.

32

Let the pitch of the club head do the work. Just imagine you're going to hit a low flat one.'

Lonnie tried another. It lofted high, came down and put on the brakes.

'Hey now!' Lonnie said.

The next one worked the same way. And the next. 'Fifteen bucks an hour I give that schnook at the club, and you do me more good in three minutes than he does in the whole hour.'

'Lonnie!' the girl called.

'Shut up!' he shouted. He slammed another one, putting more meat behind it. The girl stood where she was, and Teed saw at once that she had lost track of the ball.

'Fore!' Teed yelled.

The girl tried to break away, her hands going up. It was like slow motion. She ducked directly into the path of the ball, and he saw it rebound high from her dark head, heard the 'tok' sound it made.

The girl sat down, hard and flat, both hands flat on the top of her head. Lonnie started rolling on the grass, hugging his stomach and making strangled noises. 'Funniest . . . Jesus . . . Oh, oh, oh,' he gasped.

Teed hurried down the slope. The girl still sat there holding her head, her face all screwed up. Between sobs she was spewing out a stream of gutter language that threatened to sear the green grass for yards around.

Teed squatted on his heels. 'I guess I didn't yell in time,' he said.

She looked at him as though seeing him for the first time. She slowly lowered her hands. 'It wasn't . . . your . . . fault.' Her mouth was trembling.

She looked beyond him and Teed heard Lonnie approaching. Her eyes hardened. 'Dammit,' she said, 'it isn't enough I got to chase balls like a stinkin' caddy, but you got to clobber me on the head with one.'

'Kindly shut your big loose mouth,' Lonnie said quietly. All fire left the girl's eye. She stood up meekly. Lonnie took her by the upper arm. Teed saw the whiteness come around her mouth.

'Meet Mr Teed Morrow, darling,' he said. 'Morrow, this is my secretary. Alice Trow-bridge.'

'How do you do,' she said.

'Now, you were clumsy, weren't you, darling?'

'Yes, Mr Raval.'

'Go on up to the house and take an aspirin, darling.'

He released her. Teed felt faintly ill as he saw the depth of the indentations his hard fingers had made in her arm. She walked up the slope, legs slim and brown under the crisp chartreuse shorts, back straight, head lowered. She didn't begin to rub her arm until she had almost reached the garage.

'Is this just a friendly visit?' Raval asked, dark eyes dancing.

'Not likely. Mr Dennison's doctor told him he had to stop smoking cigars.'

'Is that supposed to mean something? It sounds like one of those cute cracks that mean something else.'

'Here's the cigars you sent him, Raval.' He handed the box over.

'That *I* sent him?' The surprise was just a shade too enormous, Teed decided. Lonnie took the box, hefted it. 'Must be some kind of mistake.'

'With five thousand cash in with the cigars, Lonnie. You aren't kidding me and you certainly aren't kidding Powell Dennison.'

Raval grinned. 'Come on up to the house. We can have a talk.'

'There isn't much to talk about, Lonnie.'

'Hell, I thought we had mutual interests, Morrow.'

Teed shrugged. 'Suit yourself.' They went up to the house. There was a small patio on the side opposite the drive. A glass-topped table, some wrought-iron chairs. Raval ordered Sam to bring drinks and then to pick up the golf equipment.

Teed lit Lonnie's cigarette and his own with the new lighter. The box sat on the table between them. After Sam brought the drinks, Lonnie Raval said, 'If there's five thousand in that box, it sort of puts me in a spot. I got to report all my income. Now how the hell will I report that? A gift? I don't want those Internal Revenue snoops raising hell with me and my accountants, do I?'

'Better not put it down as a gift from Dennison, Lonnie.'

'Look, fella. Get me off the spot. You can tell Dennison you gave me the dough. Keep it yourself.'

'And then someday you'll want a little harmless favour from me, Lonnie. I don't want to have a 'sold' sign on me.'

Lonnie clucked sadly. 'You guys! You Christers.'

'Must be we have you worried, Raval.'

One dark eyebrow went up a little. The eyes were liquid, wet-black, beautiful. 'Worried? Not such a good word, Morrow. You two are like maybe a pebble in my shoe. And I'm a lazy guy. I just hate to sit down and take my shoe off and shake the pebble out. Maybe I'm going to have to do it, though.'

'Maybe we won't shake out so easy,' Teed

said, trying to match Raval's casual confidence, trying not to show how much the quiet words had bothered him.

'Now that just doesn't make sense, Morrow. You and those silly goddam affidavits! Think I'm going to sit still and let you nibble on me? Take a message back to Dennison. Tell him Raval is scared of federal heat — so scared that he keeps his nose clean. Tell him Raval can find angles as far as state and local heat is concerned. And tell him that as far as a couple of amateur good-government bastards are concerned, Raval is laughing.'

'And offering money.'

Lonnie stared at him. 'I could learn to dislike you, Morrow. Tell Dennison I've got a couple of boys who are so stupid they're more trouble than they're worth. I'll set them up so Dennison can knock them over and be a hero.'

'He'll never go for that.'

'Stay in my hair and you'll both wish you never heard of this town.'

'So far it only adds up to noise. What can you do? Have us killed?'

Raval gave him a hurt look. 'Jesus, boy. You better stay out of those B movies. How long do you think I'd last if I went around killing people? Jesus!'

'I know that would be pretty crude, Raval. The point I was trying to make is that outside of killing us, there's no way of stopping us.'

'I don't know why I have to explain all this to you, Morrow. Look. You and your boss nosed around the City Engineer's office long enough to get the specs rewritten on the repaving of Grayman Street. It took most of the sugar out of that job and cost me personally twelve thousand. All right. Now suppose I was a manufacturer. Somebody starts cutting into my profit. What do I do? First I try to hire them. That doesn't work. Do I kill them? Hell, no. I look them over until I find a little button. Like a doorbell. I just push on the button.'

The man's confidence made Teed's mouth feel dry. 'But . . . '

'I take a look at a guy like you. Money doesn't seem to interest you. Maybe you've got enough. So I try something else.' He threw his head back and yelled, 'Alice! Alice, come on out here.'

'Coming!' she called, from the recesses of the house. She appeared almost immediately. She had changed from the sun-suit to a crisp white halter-back dress. She sat down in one of the chairs and said, poutingly, 'What a terrible headache I got!'

Lonnie Raval said, softly, affectionately,

'Honey-lamb, what happens if I tell you to go out there and see how much grass you can eat?'

She stared at him. 'You going crazy?'

'No. I mean, what happens if I really tell you to do that?'

She held his gaze for a long moment and then her eyes dropped. 'I guess, maybe I'd do it, Lonnie.'

'Show the man.'

'Gosh, Lonnie, I . . . '

'Show the man!'

The tall, tanned girl walked out into the yard. Raval watched her without expression. She bent over and pulled up a clump of grass. She raised it slowly and put it in her mouth, started to chew.

'OK, honey-lamb. Spit out the nasty grass. Come back and sit down. Morrow, you see what I mean? Now this girl here, she was pretty snotty to me last year. So I had to find out which button to push. You find the button, and you own the person. I own her. Anything I tell her to do, she does, don't you, baby?'

She looked down at her hands. 'Yes, Mr Raval.'

'You don't ever want to make me mad, do you?'

'No, Mr Raval!'

'Because when I get sore enough at you, you know what I'm going to do to you, don't you?'

Her voice was a barely audible whisper. 'Yes, Mr Raval.'

Lonnie smiled at Teed. 'I get a big yak out of how those newspaper guys make a big mystery out of how the Commies get those confessions. They ought to come talk to Raval!'

Teed felt ill at having witnessed this humiliation of a human being.

'Want to make a bet, Morrow?'

'What do you mean?'

'You stay in town long enough, and I'll own you too. I tell you to eat grass and you'll eat grass. I know. You're telling yourself you're a big strong guy and you'd die before you'd take orders like that. That's fairy-story stuff, Morrow. Hero stuff, like in the books. People aren't like that. You can break people. You can break anybody in the world, if you know how to go about it. If you want to be smart, just join my team. Dennison doesn't have to know. Keep the five grand. You like this little girl? Take her home with you. She'll do anything you tell her to do.'

'No, thanks!'

'She's a better piece than the Mayor's wife, Morrow!'

Teed stood up, unable to conceal his surprise.

'Man, how do you think that old fud got to be mayor? Raval keeps up on things. Raval keeps track. See, already I got a little handle on you. Already I found one button. And I'll find the button on Dennison, too. And you two gentlemen can hold hands and jump through a big hoop whenever I hold it up. Felice gave me a full report. She isn't bright. Just sort of shrewd.'

Raval looked lazily at Teed's clenched fist and said, 'It wouldn't be at all smart to take a punch at me, Morrow.'

'You won't stop us,' Teed said. He turned on his heel and left. As he rounded the corner of the house, he glanced back. The man and the girl sat placidly on the terrace. A master-slave relationship. A little medieval nightmare in a sunlit world.

He stepped on the starter. Under the hood a low whistle started. It increased in volume and pitch. It climbed up into a whistling scream that terminated in a sharp explosion. Clouds of white smoke rolled out of the vents.

The stringy little man called Sam was standing by Lonnie Raval. They were both laughing so hard they were doubled over. The girl in the white dress was standing behind the two of them, her laughter shrill above theirs. Teed yanked the bomb loose from the spark plug and threw it on the grass. He slammed the hood down. At the end of the driveway, as he slowed to make the turn, he could still hear them laughing.

Teed drove a mile before he permitted himself a small rueful grin. Raval had been all too convincing. The very casualness of his confidence had, in itself, been a weapon planned to undermine Teed's confidence. Whatever else Raval was, Teed realized he was also an expert amateur psychologist. He had thrown in the knowledge of Felice Carboy at the proper moment to obtain maximum shock value. The little demonstration of his power over the girl had been adequately sickening.

By the time he parked in the City Hall lot, most of his confidence had returned. The City Hall was of yellow brick and sandstone, with four two-storey pillars across the front. A patch of paper-littered parched grass stretched across the front, bisected by the wide walk leading to the foot-cupped concrete steps. Behind the building a roofed walk led to police headquarters.

Teed went into the Hall and up the stairs, heels clacking on the shiny metal treads, nostrils full of the stink of green floor-cleaning compound, ancient dust and the pink reek of the deodorant blocks in the urinals. Lonnie's Mint. That was what the wise ones called the Hall. Its symbol was the shine on the pants seat of a third-rate lawyer. Justice was blindfolded, but she carried no scales. In Deron she lay flat on her back in the City Hall with her knees high and the soiled toga entangled around her waist, with tireless relays of public servants making certain that she stayed that way.

Three City Hall girls came down the stairs toward him, high heels clacking, voices chattering about the weekend.

'S-s-st!' one said.

'Good morning, Mr Morrow,' they said, singsong, almost in chorus.

'Good morning, ladies,' he said.

They passed him, and when he looked back down at them they were looking up the stairs. They clutched each other and giggled shrilly.

Teed went into his office and through the connecting door into Powell's outer office where sallow Miss Anderson, a trustworthy import, was filing letters.

'He in?'

'Expecting you, Teed. But Commissioner Koalwitz is in there right now.'

'Give me a buzz when he's free, please.'

He went back out and sat at his own desk.

The green rug was scuffed down to where brown showed through the pile. One of the slanting window ventilators was missing, the other one cracked. Green steel desk with brown-black cigarette scars in the paint. Calendar from Mooten Brothers, A Funeral to Fit Every Purse. Ash-tray on the desk encircled by a miniature rubber tyre. Chair that creaked. Another office in another public building so like the ones that had gone before, the ones that would come afterward. Public buildings and pigeons. They seemed to go together. One landed on his windowsill, looked in with beady, wise glance.

'Pigeon, I don't think I'll mention Felice to the boss. Check on that?'

The pigeon shrugged and flew away.

3

A half hour after he had returned from lunch there was a phone call for him.

'Teed? Don't use my name over the line. Do you know who it is?'

'Of course.'

'Teed, I've got to see you. Same place as yesterday.'

'I thought we both chalked that one up to experience.'

'Please. I'm begging you. How soon can you get away?'

'I'll be busy all this week, honey.'

There was a long silence and he thought that she had hung up. 'Listen to me, Teed. I've been wrong. I've been wrong for a long time. I found out something today. Just an hour ago. Something that you ought to know.'

'What do you want to do? Change sides?'

'Don't sound so ... so contemptuous, Teed. I'm taking a risk, you know. The least you can do is ... '

'I saw a man this morning. He knew more than I thought he knew.'

Her tone was humble. 'I'm ... sorry about that, Teed. If I had it to do over again, I ... '

45

'If you know something you feel the City Manager should know, I suggest you make an appointment with Mr Dennison.'

'Damn you! Oh, damn you, Teed Morrow!'

'Sticks and stones may break my bones . . . '

'You think you know everything there is to know,' Felice said hotly. 'I wanted to tell you something because, in spite of what you said to me yesterday, I still think there's something decent about you. And I don't like what's planned for you.'

He held the phone a bit tighter, but made his voice casual. 'Don't get so fussed. If you really think it's that important, I'll get away as soon as I can. Another hour or so here, and then an hour's drive. O.K.?'

She sighed. 'That's better, Teed. Much better. I'll leave now, and I'll be there waiting for you.'

The phone line clicked dead before he could break in again. He hung up slowly. Maybe she had gotten hold of something. Something too strong for her stomach. He shrugged. He was a fool if he did, and a fool if he didn't.

He turned back to the prints and specifications of the sewer job completed by the Lantana Brothers Construction Company in 1950. The construction company was a partnership and it was common rumour, though unproven, that Lonnie Raval was the silent senior partner. Powell wanted Teed's opinion on whether it would be worth while to bring in an outside inspector to check the job and find out just how many corners had been cut. It had been an eight-hundred-thousand-dollar job, specifying the digging up of old pipe, replacing it with new pipe at a deeper level. City inspectors had been on the job as it was performed, but Teed knew that in Deron that meant less than nothing. If pipe of the cheapest quality in the proper diameter had been used, and the line hadn't been deepened, the job might have cost Lantana Brothers four hundred thousand. But it was going to be awfully tough to bring in an outside expert and expect him to dig holes in the street without anyone noticing it.

He scribbled on the bottom of Powell's memo. 'Why don't we save it until we've got them on the run and can do it openly?'

At a few minutes after three he checked out with Powell, left the office and headed for the lake. He pushed the car hard and made it in fifty minutes. Felice's convertible was parked on the narrow lane. He parked beside it.

The first thing he saw when he went in was the neat arrangement of Felice's clothes on the cane-bottom chair. She was nude on the bed, one corner of the Indian blanket flipped across her.

She raised her deeply tanned arms, her eyes smiling. 'Hello, darlin',' she said huskily. 'You made me wait so terribly long.'

He stood six feet from her. He took a cigarette out, tapped it on the new lighter, hung it in the corner of his mouth and lit it. She lowered her arms when she got tired.

'I thought you had something to tell me.'

'That can wait, can't it, darlin'?' She raised her leg and kicked the flap of blanket aside, lay watching him with her eyes almost closed.

In spite of himself he felt desire twist within him, a slow oily shifting. His hand trembled a bit as he lifted the cigarette to his mouth. To gain the necessary control, he turned his back on her, walked over to the bureau, flicked the ashes into the tray.

'What's wrong, Teed?'

'When things are finished, I like them to stay finished. If you've got anything to say, say it. If not, get your clothes on and go home.'

'Teed, I . . . '

He tensed and raised a hand. 'Shut up. Listen!'

The car had slowed on the highway. The camp and the two parked cars were not visible from the highway. He heard the faint whimper of rubber on the hard surface, the change of motor noise, and knew that the car was turning in.

There was no need to warn Felice. She scrambled out of the bed, snatched up her clothes. She darted, ludicrous in frightened nudity, toward the bathroom. A shoe fell and she dodged back, snatched it up, biting hard on her under lip, her eyes wide and scared. He took her purse and gloves and glasses off the bureau, stopped the door as she started to slam it, shoved the articles into her arms and pulled the door shut.

He took a deep breath and walked slowly toward the door. The car had stopped in the blocked lane. Two men got out, came quickly toward him. He stared hard at them and wanted to laugh, yet something choked off the laughter. In the shaped rubber masks that covered their heads, they looked like twins. Familiar twins. And then he realized that the masks represented Mortimer Snerd, he of the buck teeth, receding chin, owlish, harmless, stupid stare. And the automatic that one held, glinting oily blue in the afternoon sunlight, seemed to beam toward him a ray of cold invisible light. The light was focused on his belly and the spot it touched was cold.

The twin Snerds came close. A whisper cannot be identified or remembered. 'Turn around and walk in slow.'

'So she set this up for you? Where's your camera, boys?'

He walked in, heard the quick rustle of movement behind him and tried to move quickly forward, away from the expected blow. It hit the back of his head and it was oddly like one of the tumbles of childhood, where the skull raps smartly against the unforgiving sidewalk. He rocked toward the wall on drunken joints and they grabbed him expertly. Every touch hurt and he cried out as they twisted him, flung him onto the bed. As he started to recover, to bring into play that massive strength that he knew how to use, he was rapped again, driven down right to the edge of blackness like a kite that dives toward the earth only to recover at the last moment, struggle painfully back up. When he tried to use his arms again, he found that his wrists had been lashed to the two bedposts. He tried to kick, but it was like kicking under water, and they tied his ankles quickly.

The twin masks hovered over him, swaying like comic balloons. His head was steadied and glass grated against his lips. Warm whisky filled his mouth and his nose was clamped, a hand fastened tightly across his lips. He had to swallow in order to breathe. Twice he managed to blow the liquor out of his mouth, but time after time he was forced to swallow.

Alcoholic skyrockets exploded in the back of his mind. There was a faraway commotion, a woman's shout of anger or pain, but it was of no importance.

There was a whisper that said, 'Slower, or he'll heave it.'

Liquor roared behind his eyes, like a train in a tunnel. The tunnel began to slant downward toward the bowels of the earth. The train rushed on, faster and faster, out of control, rocking on the tracks, whistle shrilling, heading for the final and inevitable . . .

★   ★   ★

He woke up in shuddering, cold-sweat darkness. He sat up, spinning, liquor-sick. His mouth was a loose numb area. The bed swung twice, slowly, the way a pitcher winds up, and then did a gut-wrenching outside loop, spilling him out onto the harsh grass rug that scraped his face and his naked hip. Grass rug. That meant the camp. Damn fool to get so stinking. How did it happen? He went slowly across the rug on his hands and knees. It was cold. He shivered violently, but could not stop sweating. His head butted the doorframe. He turned a bit to the left and crawled out onto the porch, spreading out with his naked chest on the cold boards, his head over the edge of the porch. He fingered the back of his tongue and was sick, wrenchingly, agonizingly, meagerly. He lay for a time, panting with exhaustion, then crawled back to the door. With his fingers on the doorframe he pulled himself erect. When the camp swung dizzily, he hung onto the doorframe with all his strength, his eyes tightly shut. When it steadied a bit, he reached around the frame, opening the door with his arm, finding the light switch.

Light exploded against the windy night. He stared in at the naked woman on the floor near the bathroom door. Her back was toward him, legs drawn up.

'Got drunk with old F'lice,' he said out loud.

He blundered through the doorway, lost his grip on the frame. The camp tilted and he ran across the room, big arms flailing. His shoulder smashed against the back of the single overstuffed chair, and he went over with it, smashing a table, hitting his elbow painfully against the wall.

He sat up, rubbing his elbow. 'Take it easy,' he said. He grinned. 'Who shoved me? You shove me, Felice?' He looked at her. Now he could see her face. Her dark horrid face, her staring eyes completely white-rimmed, the blackened tongue swollen so that it held the jaw open. Like a face you make to scare people. A face to send kids screaming to mamma.

'Cut it out, F'lice,' he said petulantly.

He crawled over to her. He put his hand on her hip. It took long seconds for the chill message to come back from his hand, crescendo in his brain. He pulled his hand back and stared at it. 'Felice is dead,' he said, forming the words precisely with his numbed lips.

Got to think. Got to figure out what happened. Got to get sober, boy. Sober up fast. Shower. No, the lake. Colder and faster. Come on, boy. Get into that water.

He fell twice on the way down the path. When he got to the dock he made no attempt to dive. He merely walked off the end. He floundered clumsily, and slowly precision came back to his muscles. When he hauled himself, gasping and shivering, up onto the dock, the memory of the two Snerds slid quickly into his mind. He walked up the path. His car was there. Hers was gone.

He walked in and closed the door. He was still unsteady on his feet, still nauseated, yet his mind was beginning to work. Choice one — get dressed and drive to the nearest phone and report it to the troopers.

'Yes, sir, two men wearing Mortimer Snerd masks came in and . . . '

How nice that would be! Teed Morrow and the mayor's wife. Teed Morrow, still too loaded to walk anybody's chalk line. That would be dandy. A nice slap across the mouth for Powell Dennison. A scandal so fat and juicy that Powell's findings in regard to municipal graft would have all the effect of a penny whistle in a whirlwind.

Somebody knew she was coming out to the lake. Somebody knew he was meeting her there. And, to make the frame nice and tight, it was equally obvious that someone else was due to arrive and find him still out like a light, the body on the floor.

He trotted out and got in his car, swung it around without turning the lights on, backed it carefully down to the porch. He opened the trunk compartment and left the lid up.

Touching her was more difficult than he had thought it would be. Though most of her body was flaccid, there was the beginning of stiffness in her arms and legs. When the lid was up, the trunk light was on. He tried to move too quickly through the doorway with her, and one of her ankles rapped smartly, sickeningly on the doorframe. He shut his jaw hard, turned her legs a bit, and walked out with her, down the porch steps. He put her on her side on the floor of the trunk, facing out, then pushed the body back as far as it would go. He found that by bending her knees, he could wedge her bare feet in the corner just in front of the upright spare tyre.

Her clothes, ripped and torn in removal, were in a clutter on the bathroom floor. He picked them up, mentally checking off each item to make certain he had everything. Her suit was lime yellow, the blouse white, the shoes of yellow canvas with cork platform soles. The heavy glasses were in her purse. He put all her belongings in the trunk compartment with her. As he lowered the lid the trunk light went out and he no longer had to look at her expression of fixed, horrid surprise, at her bruised throat.

He moved the car fifty feet from the porch, still in darkness, and then went back into the camp. He held his feet in the shower to remove the grime and then inspected his clothes. They had been removed as brutally as hers. He dressed quickly in khaki trousers, flannel shirt, leather jacket. Once dressed he righted the fallen chair, carefully picked up the pieces of the ruined table, put them in the fireplace and crammed paper under them, then lit it. He dumped the three red-smeared cigarette butts on top of the flames.

He was making his third inch-by-inch

inspection of the camp for anything that might have been overlooked when he heard the car and saw the headlights swing into the lane. He walked out onto the porch, squinting into the lights, forcing himself to smile.

'Who is it?' he called when the motor had been turned off. The car lights went off.

'Seward from *Deron Times*, Morrow. We had a hell of a time finding this place. Been wandering around these hills for hours.'

Two men appeared in the light from the open doorway. One of them, a fat stranger, had a big camera case slung over his shoulder. Teed recognized the other, a slim, sharp-featured leg man from the *Times* named Ritchie Seward. He was on the City Hall beat. It was largely due to the editorials and features in the *Times* that enough public feeling had been aroused to force through the new City Manager-Mayor form of government for Deron.

'What cooks, boys?' Teed asked, trying to make his voice less thick.

Seward came up on the porch and shook hands. 'Damn if I know, Morrow. I got an anonymous tip that you could break a big story for us tonight. It was a hell of a dull night. Wife's gone to a hen party. So I picked up Carl Engalund here and we came out. Don't tell me it was for nothing!'

'I don't know anything hot, Seward,' Teed said. 'Come on in and have a drink anyway.'

Teed stumbled slightly as he followed them through the door. Seward turned and gave him a bright-eyed stare as Engalund went over to warm the seat of his pants at the fire. 'Little ahead of us, aren't you, Morrow?'

Teed grinned. 'A little, I guess. Been having a private celebration. Yesterday was my birthday.'

Engalund said, 'Hell of a thing. A setup like this and you make it a private party. What's the matter with that City Hall quail, Mr Morrow?'

'Too close to the flagpole, Carl. Bourbon all right, with plain water?'

'Fine.'

The kitchen adjoined the living room. Teed dropped a glass. It smashed on the floor. As he kicked the pieces aside, he saw Seward staring out at him with bright-eyed speculation. Teed made two drinks and took them in. 'I'm sitting this round out, boys.'

Seward sat on the bed. Engalund took the overstuffed chair. Teed sat on the cane-bottomed chair, straddling it.

Seward took a long pull at his drink. 'How is the battle going in the Hall?' he asked.

Teed shrugged. 'We're nibbling at them. I don't know how worried Raval is, though.'

'A guy like Raval,' Seward said, staring down into his drink, 'you've got to remember where he came from, how he climbed his little ladder. He drew two years in reform school and that made him smart. He's never even been booked since. He's proud of that, Teed. Like those famous television stars, Costello and Adonis, he wants to look and act legitimate.'

'What are you trying to say?'

'Just this. A pocketbook pinch doesn't hurt that rascal half as much as public condemnation as a crook. He bought his way into the Sandoval Golf Club. Goes to Miami every winter. Keeps his twin daughters in a plush private school. Now Raval knows and I know and you know, Teed, that all you can do to him is cut him down a little. Like a weed in the garden. He'll grow back. You can force him out of power in city government, and he'll still have a fine fat take off fifty other things. And when you and Dennison get tired or move on, Raval will climb up into the saddle again. I'm being practical, not cynical. So why won't he stand still for it? You can't hurt him badly.'

'Won't he stand still for it?'

'Of course not. He's got delusions of decency, Teed, and he'll become very indecent before he'll stand still for a public smear. I've been watching him a long time. We had a guy in town, Jaimey Bell. Jaimey Bell owned a tavern with a back room full of slots and a crap table upstairs. Nothing fancy. He told a reporter from the *Times* that he was going to testify before the grand jury and that he was going to name a certain big shot in town. Now everybody knew who he was going to name as the guy he had to split with. It wouldn't have hurt Lonnie a bit. The money went through too many hands before it got to Lonnie's. But it would have meant a certain notoriety.

'Jaimey was sitting at his kitchen table at midnight drinking a glass of milk and somebody shoved a shotgun through the kitchen screen and blew half his head off.'

Teed forced a smile. 'A warning, I take it?'

'With you and Dennison, Lonnie can't be that crude. But he can be very ingenious. You know why I came fifty miles on an anonymous tip?'

'Why?'

'I thought some of Lonnie's people had set you up to be knocked over. Maybe a morals rap. Something like that. If so, I was going to try to do my best to cover you, because the future of our fair city is damn important to me and you're Dennison's right hand. I'm glad I was wrong. So I'm saying this, Teed.

Watch yourself. Please watch yourself. Don't give them an opening. Any kind of an opening. Don't even get a parking ticket if you can help it. That station house is full of people who would like to bounce you off the walls until you confess you started the Chicago fire.'

'I'll . . . be careful,' Teed said. For a moment he was tempted to tell what had happened. But that was something Ritchie Seward couldn't cover up, and Teed couldn't explain adequately enough to convince even the most sympathetic cop.

'Bottoms up, Carl,' Seward said, setting his empty glass aside. He stood up. 'Thanks for the drink, Teed.'

Teed stood up too. 'Would you do me a favor, Ritchie?'

'Sure thing.'

'I think I'll stay out here tonight. That will make me a little late getting in in the morning. I'll go to an appointment I have at the courthouse instead of direct to the Hall. Would you please phone Dennison in the morning and let him know?'

'Glad to.'

Teed stood on the porch as they swung around and drove out, heading back toward the city. He waved, and when they were out of sight, he sat down on the porch steps and buried his face in his hands. He took deep, shuddering breaths. Only luck had kept them from arriving much earlier. In a way it was an omen. Perhaps the luck would hold. He wondered what had become of Felice's car, and why they had driven it away. Maybe to make it look as though she had come with him in his car.

He had to complete the rest of it. Finish out the run. He got into his car and, leaving the camp lights on, drove at a carefully legal rate of speed down to the city. At the north edge of the city he turned right, drove down through the mill area, past the railroad yards. He parked in shadows near the city dump, his lights out. He was on a back street, a barren street without houses. A smouldering dump fire made a drifting stench. The street was a block from the main highway, and high enough above it so that garish billboards screened the dump, showed their illuminated message to the speeding night traffic. A paper girl with impossible breasts and ripe smile of seduction endlessly poured beer from a misted bottle into a stemmed glass. A wild-eyed rabbit raced forever across a highway, illustrating the fleetness of a gasoline.

On the far side of the highway, on a hill, were six radio towers. The red lights outlining skeletal structures were unblinking. The six top lights blinked on and off in puzzling, off-beat cadence. The cold steering wheel was sticky under his hands as he sat there.

He remembered the damnable trunk light. As soon as he lifted the lid it was going to go on. He pulled the hood release, opened the hood, used the blade of his pocketknife to pry one terminal off the battery. Then when he opened the trunk, lifting it high, no light went on. She was in darkness. He took the clothes and the purse first, walked quickly around behind the high billboards. Far on the other side of the city a revolving beacon at the airport swept quickly, faintly across him at regular intervals. A can rolled under his foot. He scattered the torn clothes, emptied the purse on the cinders. The sweeping light touched the blackrimmed glasses and he smashed the lenses under his heel. The light touched the familiar red billfold. He took the thin sheaf of bills out of it, rubbed his palms on it to smear prints, tossed it aside. He took the cork-soled shoes, moved back and found damp earth that would take an impression. Wearing the shoes on his hands, he bent over and made two clear prints in a moist place before throwing the shoes toward the scattered clothing.

The body had stiffened a great deal. It

seemed far heavier than before. As he tried to lower it gently, it slipped out of his wet hands and fell heavily. The sweeping light touched her face for an instant and he knew that he would never forget it. He tore her watch from her wrist and could not force himself to try to remove her rings. He found a rusted tin can. He pushed the bills and watch into it. He bent the lid back, then threw the can as far into the dump as he could. It hit with a thin sound lost in the noise of a freight going by. He wiped his wet hands on the thighs of the khaki trousers and walked blindly back to the car, remembering to stay out of the billboard lights. He left behind him the tanned body that had been so precise in love-making, the eyes that had been watchful, the lips that had kissed his.

Teed fixed the battery terminal and got behind the wheel. The paper girl smirked at him. The rabbit watched him with Ritchie Seward's bright eyes. The red lights beat out an inaudible rhythm.

When he was a mile from the camp the rain started. He turned out the lights, undressed in darkness, slid quickly into an exhausted sleep that was like death itself.

4

At nine o'clock Teed went into Powell Dennison's private office.

Powell said, with a smile, 'Glad you changed your mind, Teed. Seward gave me your message a few minutes ago. Did you drive in last night.'

'No. I drove in this morning. Did Seward tell you why he was out there?'

'Some kind of an anonymous tip, he said.'

Teed walked over and closed the door. He came back and sat by the desk. 'That's what I want to talk to you about, Powell. Something funny is going on, and I don't know just what it is. Yesterday afternoon I got a phone call from Mrs Carboy, the mayor's wife. She was pretty mysterious. Said she had something to tell me. Hinted that it was hot, and she didn't want to come openly here to your office and tell you. I suggested some place in town and she said that it had better be outside town. So I told her how to get to the camp.'

'What did she have to say?'

'That's the point. She never did show up. That's why I stayed out there, hoping she

64

would. Maybe Seward was supposed to find her out there.'

'That would make a nice little scandal, wouldn't it? She's an attractive woman.'

'Do you think she could have anything for us, Powell?'

Dennison pursed his lips. 'That's hard to say. Mark Carboy is not, I believe, permitted to know the inside workings of the Raval group. He is an earnest, stupid, clumsy, dishonest man, perfectly content to follow orders. But he might know something important. And I imagine that if he knew it, his wife would know it. Maybe something came up that kept her from keeping the appointment. Or maybe she was merely acting on orders, trying to frame you with Seward. Better try to get in touch with her, Teed.'

'Do you think that's smart? If she's sincere about this, it might put her on a spot.'

'Let me think for a moment.' Powell shoved his chair back from his desk, crossed his heavy legs, tapped his upper lip with a pencil.

'Maybe,' Powell said, 'if Miss Anderson could phone from the drugstore, so it wouldn't go through the Hall switchboard.'

'And say what?'

'Say that it will be all right to make a new appointment for today for the one she missed yesterday. She ought to catch on. Then you can go back out to the lake and wait for her.'

'OK,' Teed said, as though pleased with the suggestion.

'You instruct Miss Anderson, please.'

The sallow woman listened carefully, nodded, walked out. Teed went in to wait with Powell. Miss Anderson was back in five minutes. She looked more pallid than usual.

'Mr Dennison, there's some sort of trouble. A maid, I believe it was, answered the phone. She was weeping and incoherent. I heard the gossip as soon as I got back in the building. Something about the Mayor going to identify the body.'

Dennison doubled a big fist and hit the desk so hard the desk lighter jumped and toppled over. 'By God! It sounds like this might be what we need. Teed, run over to police headquarters. Find out what you can and come right back.'

Teed walked through the covered passage-way with long strides. A uniformed patrolman and a pasty man who was chewing a kitchen match stood talking in low tones to the desk sergeant behind his wire grilled window.

As Teed walked up they all stared at him, the blank, flat, unmeaning stare of the wise cop looking at the political amateur.

'Mr Dennison's secretary reported some

sort of rumour going around about the Mayor. Has he had an accident?'

The pasty man shoved his grimy felt hat back, worked the match over to the opposite corner of his mouth. 'You work for Dennison, eh?'

'Yes. My name is Morrow.'

'And you're bird-dogging for Dennison, eh?'

Teed controlled his annoyance. 'He sent me down here to find out if there had been an accident.'

The man with the match turned to the sergeant. 'George, you think that was an accident?'

George scratched his semibald head. 'You know, Harry, I think the fella did it on purpose. That's what I think.'

The pasty one had a rasping laugh. 'George, sooner or later we're going to make a cop out of you. Friend, the Mayor's lady got herself knocked off. She got stripped and robbed and raped and strangled, and some kids found her body on the city dump this morning about an hour and a half ago. That answer your question?'

'Do they know when it happened?'

'With a body out on a cold night, it's kind of hard to tell. It happened some time before midnight, they think. Lonely neighbourhood up there. Hizzoner has gone down to the morgue to make the formal identification.'

'Who'd do a thing like that?'

The uniformed cop shrugged. 'I was on the four to eight. I covered her up with a tarp outa the prowl until Homicide could get there.' He frowned as though to get something straight in his mind. 'She wasn't now what you'd call stacked. But nice. Plenty nice.' He made a loud lip-smack and shook his head fondly.

'Sure you didn't crawl under that tarp with her, Distom?' George asked.

Distom stiffened. 'Now that's a hell of a thing to say,' he said indignantly. 'What do you think I am?'

George ignored him. 'Didn't you know her, Harry?' he asked the pasty one.

'Know her! Hell, I and Buster Young guarded the presents at their wedding. Let's see. Four years ago. The Mayor give us twenty bucks apiece. He wasn't mayor then, you know. He was Commissioner of Public Safety. That was under Mayor Kennelty. You know, I was wondering at that time what a dish like that was marrying Carboy for. You couldn't tell about her when she had those glasses on, but she took them off at the reception. Had a gleam in her eye then, George. And walked like a cat. I say some

68

punks prob'ly yanked her into a car right off the sidewalk, not knowing who she was, and took her out there to the dump. I'd say prob'ly some hopped-up kids and . . . '

He seemed suddenly to remember that Teed was still standing there.

'That all you want to know, Morrow?'

'Yes, thanks.'

'Don't mention it.'

He walked away, aware that they were staring at his back, that as soon as he had left they would add comments about the City Manager and his office boy. He walked back up to Dennison's office, full of enormous relief, and told Dennison the story.

At eleven o'clock the *Times* had an extra on the street, the front page a replate of the previous evening edition.

Miss Anderson brought two copies up to the office. Teed put his heels on the desk and tilted back in his chair. They had used a wedding picture of her, veil and all. BRUTAL MURDER OF MAYOR'S WIFE. Nude body discovered at seven-thirty this morning in the city dump a few yards behind the Thorman Street billboards. Mayor hospitalized for shock after viewing remains.

The newspaper's factual coverage had the effect of making Teed feel as though he had no part in it. In some alien dream he had left

69

a body where this one had been found. The newspaper coverage, was, between the lines, outraged, semi-hysterical.

Teed wondered how two men would take it, two men who had worn the Snerd masks, had left her dead in the camp. And the man who had given them their orders — this would be a bit of a shock to him, also.

★   ★   ★

'Dr P. K. Muriel, coroner, stated that the murdered woman had been criminally attacked. The police laboratory examination disclosed two clues. One was a smear of grease on the body which apparently could not have come from any object in the area in which the body was discovered. This, police state, indicates that the body, in a nude condition, was transported from the scene of the crime to the city dump, possibly in the trunk compartment of an automobile. The severely crushed condition of the throat indicates that great strength was used. The second clue which has not yet been explained is a scrap of thin rubber, painted red on one surface, found wedged under one of the murdered woman's fingernails. Police state that there are further clues which they do not wish to reveal at this time. Deputy Chief

Wallace Wetzelle, formerly Homicide Captain, has personally taken charge of the case at the request of Public Safety Commissioner Koalwitz.'

Teed put the paper down. That note about the trunk of the car had been like catching a hammer blow between the eyes. It dazed him. The rain had taken out the tracks he had improvised. He remembered the bright-red bulbous cheeks of the Snerds. Felice had evidently clawed at one of them, torn a small hole in the rubber.

It had not been enough for them to kill her. They had to attack her first. He wondered if that had been in the script. Probably. Anything to make him look as evil as possible; anything to lose him the maximum amount of sympathy.

There was an inevitability about the pictures that unreeled in the back of his mind. Hired witnesses who would testify that Mrs Carboy had told them she was going to West Canada Lake to see Mr Teed Morrow. Other hired witnesses who would say that they had seen Morrow's car in town at such and such an hour last night. Seward's testimony that Morrow had been drunk. And somebody would find the can containing the money and the watch. That would blow the robbery motive all to hell.

71

She had driven to the lake in daylight. Somebody would have recognized her on the road. He brought his feet down onto the floor. The scheme, which had seemed so bright during darkness, now seemed incredibly stupid. A man who could hire others to kill could easily hire others to bear false witness.

Maybe at this moment they were searching his apartment, finding that photo he had taken of her just two weeks ago. A damn fool trick that had been. In the picture she was standing on the dock, ready to dive, smiling back at him over her shoulder. He'd destroyed her notes, had never written her any. But that picture . . .

With sudden nervous energy he got up, told Miss Anderson he'd be back after lunch. Horace Dey, an affable, talkative little man on the Board of Assessors, cornered Teed at the foot of the stairs and Teed had to be rude in order to pry himself free after five nerve-racking minutes. He sped out of the lot and proceeded to hit every traffic light red on the way to Bannock Road. The development was a quiet area of wide grass, small, pleasant brick buildings. The playground was full of pre-school toddlers. He pulled up in front of his own doorway.

He opened the car door and then froze.

The car parked directly ahead of his, the car that he had only half-noticed, was Felice's shabby convertible.

Teed forced himself to break out of the trance. He walked woodenly to his doorway and unlocked his door. He crossed the small, attractive living room and went into the bedroom. He yanked open the top left bureau drawer, took out the thin stack of photographs. The one of Felice was the third one in the stack. He went through the rest of them. In a shot of the camp the back of her car was visible. The others were all right. He burned the two in the bathroom, dropping them into the toilet when the flame reached his fingers. The laundry bag was hanging on the back of the closet door. He dumped it out, found one handkerchief with a smear of her lipstick on it. A police lab could easily prove through spectroscopic analysis that it was her brand. To burn it would make too much of a stench. With nail scissors, he cut the handkerchief hem in a half-dozen places. He ripped it into strips, ripped the strips into squares and flushed the ragged squares down the toilet after the charred fragments of the pictures.

What else? Her perfume on his clothes? Not likely. And she had never been in his apartment, only at the camp. He knew that the camp needed a more thorough inspection than he had been able to give it on the previous night.

And now, the problem of the car. Doubtless the police were searching for it all over the city. Probably Mrs Kidder had noticed it parked near his doorway. Mrs Kidder noticed everything. The car had been there at dawn, probably. And Mrs Kidder would assume that Teed had been in, that he had had a guest, possibly feminine.

The worst thing he could do would be to attempt to sneak the car away. He knew that. Too many people had seen it. Too many would remember it later. To recognize it officially as Mrs Carboy's, or merely to complain to Mrs Kidder about people parking in front of his door. That was the question. Whoever had planned the frame had done a neat job. A man had very probably parked it just after dusk, walked unhurriedly away. Dead woman found with Morrow. Dead woman's car found at Morrow's apartment. How did the car get there, Morrow? I don't know, sir. What do you mean, you don't know? Did she bring it there? Did she come to meet you there? And you suggested a little ride in your car. A nice ride out into the hills, Morrow. And you took her to your camp, didn't you? And when you got tight she fought off your advances and so you killed her, didn't you?

'No,' he said aloud. 'No, I didn't.'

He dug his fingers into his scalp. How to handle it. He snapped his fingers, sat down at the alcove table, looked up the *Times* number, gave it to Mrs Kidder at the desk. She put the call through quickly.

'Seward isn't here right now. Hold it a minute. I'm wrong. He's just coming in.'

'Ritchie? This is Teed Morrow. Remember our little talk last night? You said you'd cover me if anybody tried anything funny. Listen to this. I stayed at the lake, went directly to the office this morning. Just came back here to my place. Yes, I live in the Bannock Road Garden Apartments. Number eleven. Second building on the left of the main drive after you go through the gates. Know what I found in front of my door? A '46 Pontiac convertible. Grey. A little beat. I'm not sure, but I think it belongs . . . belonged to Mrs Carboy.'

Seward whistled softly. 'Now, isn't that something.'

'It goes with something I maybe should have told you last night. I was expecting her out at the lake. She wanted to spill something about her husband, the Mayor. She never showed. I was afraid she'd come while you were there and you'd jump to the wrong conclusion. You can check with Dennison on that.'

Seward's voice turned crisp. 'Do you think she was killed because she was going to talk to you?'

'I didn't think so. Not until I noticed this car here. Maybe it isn't even hers. But suppose it is. And suppose the police find out that she was going to come and see me. Add that to the body being transported, they think, in a trunk compartment, and where does it leave me? You're the guy who said I should even avoid parking tickets.'

'You sound a little rattled, Morrow.'

'Hell, wouldn't you be?'

'Maybe I would. Look, don't get smart and try to drive that car away from there.'

'I wouldn't touch that car.'

'Good. You sit tight. You read about Deputy Chief Wetzelle taking over the case?'

'Yes, I did. What does that mean?'

'I don't know yet. Koalwitz pressured it through. Koalwitz doesn't spit unless Raval tells him to. And Wetzelle took the case away from Captain Herb Leighton, present Homicide captain and the only square-shooting captain on the force. So that gives me an idea. I'll pick up Leighton and come on out there. You wait for us, hear?'

'I'll be right here.'

After he hung up, Teed took out a handkerchief and wiped his sweating face. Ritchie Seward arrived in twenty-five minutes. With him was a cadaverously tall man Teed recognized as having seen around the Hall. Herb Leighton's handshake was limp, damp and cold. He looked vaguely like a shaven Lincoln, and his thin high voice furthered the impression.

'Her car,' Leighton said when the introductions were over. 'Checked the number again when Ritchie phoned me.' He stared at Teed out of deep-set eyes so lifeless that they looked as if the pupils were dusty. He folded his long bones into a chair. His knees stuck up sharply. He gave the impression of having some chronic disease that left his energy at a low ebb. When he yawned Teed saw that his teeth were tiny, like a child's.

'Somebody fixing to clobber you, Morrow.' It wasn't a question.

'It seems that way.'

'She was a busy woman. Least since Mark married her. Pretty sure I knew three boys who bedded her down.' He counted them off slowly on languid fingers, yellowed by nicotine. 'Lonnie Raval. Luke Koalwitz. Judge Kennelty. Heard 'em comparing notes at the Lantana Brothers picnic last summer. Sort of had a hunger for the mature type, I guess.' He smiled without mirth. 'Covering the City Hall beat, Rich, did you get to cover that too?'

Seward, astonishingly, blushed. 'I was out there one day trying to get an interview with Carboy. That was when he was staying out of sight on account of that bus-franchise squabble. He wasn't home, but she was. After about ten minutes I suddenly realized I was going to get myself into a position where I'd have to write nice things about the Mayor, just to ease my conscience. So I got out of there fast. I think she was a little peeved at me.'

Leighton turned his deep-eyed dusty stare on Teed. 'Figuring it out, boy, I'd say she'd fling her tail at anybody who'd either do Mark good, or do him less harm. So I'm sort of putting you on the list too. Mind?'

Teed made himself grin. 'And I was thinking it was my personal charm. OK, Captain. If you're going to try to help, I might as well come clean. Add me to that list.'

Seward looked at him with something close to contempt and turned away.

Leighton said softly, 'I suppose you took her up to that camp.'

'She would come up by herself and meet me there. Weekend afternoons, and then only since the other camps have been closed.'

Seward stood looking out the windows, his hands behind him, rocking back and forth from toe to heel.

'She try to pump you? Find out what Dennison is planning?'

'In a subtle way. I never told her anything. We broke up . . . a while back when she tried to tell me to take it easy on her husband.'

'I suppose people saw her driving up there and back.'

'I don't know.'

Leighton sighed. 'Seward seems to think I'm willing to go out on a limb for you, Morrow.'

'I'm not so sure now,' Seward snapped, not turning.

'It ain't a moral issue, Ritch,' Leighton said softly. 'It's a murder situation. They keep me on the cops, boy, so they can look at my beat-up clothes and my old heap of a car and my goddam mortgage and they can say, 'See, we got an honest officer on the force here in Deron'. So I keep my nose reasonably clean, Morrow. When I go out on a limb, I don't want any son of a bitch sawing it off close to the trunk. Now stop looking at the rug and look at my eyes, Morrow. Did you kill her?' His voice sounded like two files being rubbed together.

'No. I didn't kill her.'

'Was she out at your camp last night with you messing around with her?'

'No.'

'She gave you any little keepsakes that could tie the two of you together?'

'No.'

'They liable to find anything of yours among her stuff?'

'Not a thing.'

He pulled himself slowly out of the chair. 'I don't condemn you on moral grounds, Morrow. Better men than you and me have done like that little old dog on the railroad tracks. I just think it was damn poor judgment for a man in your position to fediddle the Mayor's wife.'

'I know that, now.'

'I think they'll try to hurt Dennison through you. Hurt what he's trying to do. I don't like having that car planted outside your place. Might be, they'll haul you in on suspicion and beat the hell out of you. Do you think you can take it?'

'I think so.'

'They'll want you to talk about everything Dennison is planning to do. No man can take it for too long. So after I arrange about this car, I'm going to talk to Armando Rogale. He's a tough little wop lawyer and a fighter. And he knows his way around. Soon as you

80

drop out of circulation I'll figure they're hiding you in one of the precincts, and I'll stick Armando on 'em. Anybody asks you, he's your lawyer.'

'What are you going to do about the car?' Morrow asked.

Captain Leighton looked at him blandly. 'Why, I'm going to check this whole place and see if I can find out who left it there. With any luck I'll cover the whole area before it's officially found. And then I'll phone it in myself. If they jug you and Armando can't get you out, Ritch here will stick the *Times* on the force. So figure that all you have to do is keep your mouth shut for not more than six or eight hours of pummelling. They won't be stupid enough to try to charge you with her murder. Isn't enough to go on.'

He ambled slowly out, pulling the door shut behind him.

'Like him?' Seward asked.

'He's an odd man, isn't he?'

'He wears very damn well, Teed. He settles a lot of department disputes, because they know he's square. He knows a surprising amount about a surprising number of people, and he never forgets anything. I saw him drunk only once. That was the day three men he'd caught were electrocuted. He talked about murder. He said, 'No human ever kills

81

another human without also killing himself'. I questioned that. I told him that a lot of people got away with it. He just gave me that tired smile and said, 'And there's a lot of dead people walking the streets'. I guess in his own way he's both a sentimentalist and an amateur mystic. I'm glad you told him the truth. He would have found out, and when he did, nothing you or I could say would make him lift a finger for you. He hates a liar.'

'He's a tough man to lie to, I imagine.'

'And a tough man to kill,' Seward said, almost with awe. 'He's got the lead that's been dug out of him. He keeps it in a glass dish on his mantel. Enough lead so that when you first see it, it looks like a little dish of candy.'

'Have lunch with me, Ritchie. Then you'll get an eyewitness report on the way I'm picked up.'

'Maybe you ought to tell Powell Dennison that you might be picked up. Maybe he'll jump the gun on all the data you people have collected.'

'And how would you know about that?'

'Dammit, Teed, this is my town. The same way it's Herb Leighton's and even Lonnie Raval's. Everybody knows that you and Dennison are hiding in your fort making up a pile of snowballs. A lot of us hope you're going to have rocks hidden in the snowballs. As long as you come out fast, you'll have people on your side. When you start to weaken, you two will be almost all alone. One thing in your favour — that's Andy Trim, the D.A. He's all wind and ambition. He's played along with Raval because that has made sense so far. If he sees a chance to dump Raval in a way that will give him a reputation all over the state, he'll do it. Come on. I'll wait while you check in with Powell, and then we'll have some food.'

He followed Teed in his car on the way back to the Hall.

5

After lunch with Ritchie Seward, Teed went back to the office and tried to work. Dennison had procured abstracts of the sheets from the Assessor's records. The current project was to check the private-home assessments of the politically faithful against the rebels. For years the Board of Assessors had been one of the most potent weapons of the Raval clique. Step on the wrong toe and you start paying taxes on an assessed valuation of fifteen thousand rather than the previous five thousand. Grievance Day had become a farce.

But Teed could not keep his mind on what he was doing. He remembered the way he had awakened from the Sunday afternoon nap, content and self-sufficient. Just forty-eight hours ago. Now that precious detachment was lost and he missed it. He realized that for too many years he had been like a man in a crap game using somebody else's money. Now he was being forced to gamble with his own money, and he didn't like the sense of participation, the feeling of risk and potential loss.

He had taken pride in being able to do an honest and workmanlike job at his speciality. But always the job had been something he could toss over his shoulder at five o'clock. And smacking down the crooked ones had been a pleasure not so much from any innate sense of righteousness, but rather from joy in a good scrap. Detachment had been his armour and maybe, he thought, things had come a bit too easy. Maybe he was a very special type of flawed hero, a guy who could turn the last card without a tremble merely because nothing really important was at stake.

In that moment he envied Powell Dennison. Dennison believed with all his heart in what he was doing. And he felt guilt that Dennison presupposed a similar dedication in his right-hand man. Powell would never sell out. Teed had thought he would never sell out, either. And now . . . if the price were high enough . . . if safety were the price?

The old saw was that a man has to live with himself. But if the choice is to either live with someone you can't respect, or stop living entirely . . .

He recognized the potential danger of that train of thought, and tried to push it out of his mind.

At three o'clock Miss Anderson told him

that a Mr Armando Rogale was here to see Mr Morrow.

Rogale came bustling in. He was about thirty, a small, stocky, swaggering man wearing a beautifully cut gabardine suit. His face was pale and, except for the snapping black eyes, as expressionless as an egg. From the small, thin-lipped mouth came a rich and astonishing baritone.

He shut the door behind him, shook hands briskly, plumped himself down in the chair and stared at Teed with both amusement and speculation in the dark eyes.

'I appear to be your attorney, Mr Morrow, according to that Leighton spook.'

'I don't really know whether I'll need a lawyer, Mr Rogale.'

'We'll call this preventative medicine.'

Teed studied him. 'How come you're willing to be unpopular?'

Rogale inspected manicured nails. 'Good question. This town is a jungle. The jackals run in a pack. You want to be a jackal, you can get along OK, if you listen to the boss jackal. I'm a porcupine. Every once in a while a jackal takes a slap at me and gets a noseful of quills. Just say I've got a porcupine temperament, Morrow. Too sharp to be swallowed. You ever see a skinny porcupine? They live pretty good.'

'Rebellion for the sake of rebellion?' Teed asked.

Rogale gave him a sharp look. 'What do you want from a lawyer? An emotional strip tease? I grew up in Deron. My old man was a carpenter, an immigrant, a professional patriot. Bill of Rights. Constitution. You know what I mean. In our ward there was a code of behaviour. No matter how bright you were, you were supposed to ask for help when you voted, just like you were illiterate. Our ward always threw every vote to the machine. My old man went to night school. He did his own voting and kept splitting his ticket. Bad example to the others. They beat him up three times, and the third time they accidentally cracked his skull and he was in a coma for three weeks before he died. After I passed the bar I tried to set up in Utica, then in Syracuse. No dice. I had to come back here. Now I'm a minor irritant. Someday I want to be some sort of avenging angel — or maybe demon. Cross-examine?'

'No, thanks.'

'You and Dennison are on the hot spot. Want to hear a theory?'

'Sure.'

'Felice Carboy was a bitch. And a pretty bright gal. She tried to make a trade — her body for hubby's immunity. No dice, I imagine, from what Leighton told me. So she wanted to add a little more to her side of the scales. Something juicy. Something that would help you and Dennison. It might have been good enough so that you would be willing to make a deal with her. She actually knew more about the Raval operations here than Mark Carboy does. Maybe she trusted the wrong guy. Anyway, somebody found out. She's potentially dangerous, playing around with you. So kill her and implicate you. Two birds with one thud.'

Teed said slowly, 'That same sort of idea has been growing in the back of my mind. Her call to me came through the switchboard here, the call where she said she had something hot to tell me.'

'That could be it.'

'Her name wasn't used.'

'Nevertheless, if the girl on the board at that time recognized the voice and reported it, that girl will be a little queasy right now. It's something to work on. Look, Morrow, I'm your lawyer. It's a confidential relationship. The more I know, the more I can help. I want to be awful damn certain you didn't kill her.'

'I didn't.'

'Is there anything I should know, then?'

Teed got up and walked to the windows.

He looked out on the parking lot, at the office-building windows across the way. He came back to his chair and sat down. With an effort he kept his voice steady. He told Rogale every detail of the previous evening.

After he finished Rogale let the silence grow for long minutes. He bounced out of the chair, walked over to the wall and drove his fist against it.

'Mother of God!' he said. '*Sangre de Cristo!* Of all the fatuous idiots in the wide world, I have to offer my services to the clown prince.'

'Now, listen, Rogale! Maybe my reaction wasn't too bright, but . . .'

'Shut up! Let me think. Mortimer Snerd masks, yet. Imported talent. Guys who probably hit town Sunday and are gone now.' He held out his hand. 'Give me the key to that camp.'

Teed meekly took the key off his ring and handed it over. 'What are you going to do?'

'Clean up after you. Rinse your diapers. What do you think?'

'I checked it pretty carefully, Rogale.'

Armando heaved a great sigh and sat down. 'Look. So help me, I believe you. I believe that it happened exactly the way you said it did, and only the fates kept Seward from barging in while you were still snoring.

So, let's be practical. There's maybe five hundred nice clean fingerprints out there. Hers. Even if you tried to remove them, you wouldn't know where to look. Inside of the bathroom medicine cabinet. Thumbprint on the underside of the john lever. Maybe I'll just go out and burn the son of a bitch down. Arson, added to all my other crimes. Look, you got a girl you can take out there?'

'What do you mean?'

'If they don't pick you up this afternoon, you get yourself a girl and get out there. Play house. Settle down. I'll be through by then. She better be a girl with nothing to hide, a girl who doesn't care if the cops lift her prints. The more stuff she leaves around, the better. Lipstick, panties, hair on the hairbrush. You got one, or have I got to rent you one?'

'It seems pretty cold-blooded.'

'So is the way they electrocute a man. If they cut you when they shave your leg, they even put iodine on it. It's as cold-blooded as can be.'

'You don't have to try to scare me, Rogale. I'm already scared.'

'Can you get a girl?'

'On that short notice, no.'

'Stay here. I'll use an outside phone. I'll be back.'

Rogale was back in fifteen minutes. He said, 'This is a line of business I never thought I'd be in. A good thing I got contacts. It will cost you a hundred bucks. She'll be in the cocktail lounge at the Hotel Deron at five o'clock, ready to take off. Look in the booths on the left for a tall girl. They told me she has brown hair and her name is Miss Heddon.'

'Is she pretty?'

Armando looked at his watch. 'I better get going. You should care if she looks like a hop frog, Morrow. Don't get her out there until about six-thirty. That'll give me time.'

After Rogale had left, leaving Teed feeling dazed, he went out and cashed a cheque. When he got back Miss Anderson said that a Captain Leighton had phoned, and had left a number to call.

Leighton said, 'You get a little reprieve, Morrow. Two kids who know you because you played catch with them one Saturday afternoon happened to notice the guy who left the car. They say it wasn't you. To kids all grown-ups look alike, except the ones they know, so there's no description. You're off the hook until they figure that out.'

When Leighton hung up, it was five minutes to five. Teed went in and told Powell that he was going out to the lake again.

91

Powell looked disappointed. 'I wanted you to go over some stuff with me tonight, Teed.'

'I'd rather not go. But this is orders from my lawyer.'

'Care to explain?'

'Not quite yet Powell. I'm sorry. I'm just trying to get off the hook on this car business.'

'Tomorrow then. How about the assessment survey?'

'I'm just no good today. I didn't do over a tenth of it.'

Powell shrugged and smiled. 'OK, I won't push you.'

Teed got into his car and drove to the hotel. He found a parking space in the middle of the next block. He felt an odd flutter of excitement that ran up his spine, tingled at the nape of his neck. He could see the sense of Rogale's idea, but the artificiality of the situation bothered him. He was both repelled and intrigued by the idea of the coarse, cold-eyed creature who would be waiting for him.

The cocktail lounge had a sidewalk doorway and he walked in quickly. The bar was thronged at this hour. There were six booths along the wall at the left. Four were empty. There were three men in one of the booths, a girl sitting alone in another. She was a tall girl, and her hair was brown, but nothing else matched his conception. She wore a dark-green tailored suit, a silver fox fur, a pert green hat with a veil. Her face had a look of fragility, delicacy, and breeding.

He paused uncertainly and turned slowly toward the bar. Then, with a mental shrug, he walked quickly to the booth. 'Miss Heddon?'

Calm, deep-blue eyes and a slow smile. 'How do you do. I'm Barbara Heddon.'

He sat down awkwardly. 'Teed Morrow, Miss Heddon. I'm a little late, I guess.'

'Not very. Shall I hurry this, or do you want to order yourself a drink, Teed?'

'I'll have a drink, Barbara.' He signalled the waiter, ordered a stinger.

She was completely at ease. Her brown gloves lay across the green purse that matched her suit. Beside her cocktail glass was a silver combination cigarette case and lighter. She accepted his cigarette gravely, leaned forward for the light, holding the veil out of the way of the flame. She did not touch the rest of her cocktail until his came, then lifted her glass as he did, smiling across the rim at him.

'If you'll excuse me a moment, Teed, I have a phone call to make.'

'Of course.' After she walked away, into the lobby, tall and with a certain flair, a certain elegance, Teed sat down. He wondered if the long arm of coincidence had produced two Miss Heddons at the same time and the same place. Her tone of voice, her accent, matched her look of assurance and breeding.

She was back quickly, slipping into her side of the booth as he tried awkwardly to get to his feet.

'Another drink, Barbara?'

'Yes, thank you.'

She looked at him with a pretty frown. 'Teed, we aren't getting acquainted, are we? We're acting like a pair of European diplomats.'

'Well, you took my breath away, Barbara. God knows what I expected. Certainly not you. You're very lovely.'

For a moment there was a slightly bitter twist to her mouth. 'And you're quite willing to be seen in public with me, I suppose.'

'Sorry. I did sound pretty stuffy, didn't I?'

She smiled. 'For that touch of sympathetic imagination, Mr Morrow, I shall tell you about my phone call. I give myself an expensive luxury. It's called selectivity. I phoned to say that I was not going to develop a headache.'

'Now we're both flattered.'

'A society for mutual admiration, Teed. And thank you for not being Mr Smith.

Thank you very much for not being a Mr Smith. Very truly yours, Barbara.'

'Now a question. Is it a ... oh, a customary thing for you to be willing to go out of town like this?'

'Hardly. But you were vouched for. Highly recommended, I suppose is the right way to say it.' She smiled, and then her mood changed with surprising rapidity. 'And, of course,' she said, 'I am also filled with curiosity. You look like one of those precious and indomitable males who go around swelling out their chests and telling their less favoured brethren that they never have to pay for it.'

It was the first hint of coarseness, but the shot was very well aimed.

'Ouch,' he said. 'One of that same type must have bitten you once upon a time.'

'Now I say ouch,' she said. 'Never lead with your right, Barbara.'

'We better call a truce before somebody gets battered. Ready?'

She nodded. He paid the cheque. She had a small overnight bag on the bench beside her. He carried it out, placed it on the back seat of the car, held the car door for her.

As he got behind the wheel he said, 'Shall I leave the top down?'

'Please,' she said. She took her hat off. Her

hair was a cap of brown curls. When they drove up out of the valley the last rays of the setting sun touched her hair and brought out red touches that were like hidden flame.

'Teed?'

'Yes, Barbara.'

'What do you think of pacts?'

He grinned. 'Diplomatic, suicide? What color?'

'Pull over and stop for a minute. Let's whip up a pact.'

He stopped the car, turned to face her, his left arm resting on the top of the wheel, right arm along the seat back. She turned in the seat to face him, and all the light had gone out of her blue eyes. They looked dead, long buried.

'It is a standard gambit, Teed, that sooner or later you will ask me how I got into the oldest profession. Men seem to have a compulsion to ask that question. So, let's have a pact. Don't ask me, and you won't make it necessary for me to invent some tragic song and dance just to satisfy your curiosity. Teed, just take me for . . . granted.'

'Any pact involves a concession on both sides, Barbara. I think I probably would have asked you. Now I won't. But you have to agree to something too. You have to promise not to pretend to any emotion or any excitement that isn't genuine.'

'Aren't you being stupid? Aren't you cheating yourself, Teed?'

'How so?'

'I'm as cold as those monsters they dig out of glaciers. You're the first . . . customer I've ever told that to. Now that I've said it, I think maybe you better take me back to the hotel. I don't want to cheat you.'

'I'd rather keep on with it, Barbara, and have each of us keep our side of the pact. Maybe this will be a little platonic jaunt into the country. I really don't care, one way or the other.'

'Then don't pay me until I ask you to,' she said harshly.

'It's a deal, Barbara.'

Her smile came slowly. She rested her cheek for a moment against the back of his hand. 'Drive the car, mister.'

He drove into the first village just as the market was about to close. She came in with him and they selected steaks and frozen vegetables. He was amused by the way she watched the meat scale as the steaks were weighed.

Teed carried the bag of groceries out. It was cooler in the hills, so he put the top up.

'Barbara, a confession. Willing to listen?'

'Of course.'

'I've got a devious motive for taking you to the camp. I want you to do something for me. When we leave, I want the camp to look as though you had been there. Lipstick on the towels, bobby pins on the floor, nail polish on the bathroom shelf.'

It was too dark to see her face. 'Thanks for being honest.'

'You'll do it?'

'Of course, Teed.'

'Then there's no question of my not paying you, of course. I'm paying you for agreeing to leave your imprint on the place.'

'If you say so.' She was silent for a few minutes. 'You're using me to make someone jealous, I suppose?'

'No, Barbara.'

'Then you're using me to cover up the traces of someone else. That's the only other answer. Probably some righteous wife who can't manage to restrict it to her own bed.'

'Don't be so bitter, Barbara.'

'Why not? Aren't professionals in any field bitter about amateur competition?'

'Please don't ever tell anyone what I asked you to do.'

She laughed flatly. 'That's funny. You said that as though you believe you can actually trust me.'

'Strangely enough, I do.'

She rested her fingers lightly on his arm. 'Teed, we've got to stop hacking at each other. Got any ideas?'

'Sure. Try this idea for size. You're a girl I've known for years. I've talked you into a picnic and a moonlight swim, and we're telling each other that's all there's going to be. But I have some pretty advanced ideas, and you're wondering just how hard you're going to fight for your honour. O.K?'

'Gosh, I don't know whether I like that game or not.'

'You'll love it. Say, remember old Albert?'

'Albert?'

'Sure. The guy you stood up so you could go on the sleigh ride with me. You remember *him*!'

'Oh, Albert! The one with the pimples. The one that looked like a startled owl. Whatever happened to him?'

'He's got a job sitting on public buildings to scare away the pigeons. Making a big success of it, too.'

'I always knew Albert was going places. I just *knew* it!' she said.

She moved so close to him that her thigh was warm against his. She threw back her head and laughed with delight. In the onrushing darkness of the mountain road her laughter was young, warm, heartbreakingly vulnerable.

They discussed the mythical mutual acquaintances of their imaginary past, and then he slowed for a familiar narrow lane, shifted into second, finding to his relief that there was no car there, meaning that Rogale had finished, had left.

She carried the bag of groceries and he took the overnight case. 'Better wait at the foot of the steps until I get some lights on, Barbara.'

'Doesn't the air smell wonderful up here? I'm going to be hungry as a wolf.'

As he had hoped, Armando Rogale had left the key in the door. He found the light switch. She walked in, put the groceries on the drain board, turned and smiled at him. Once again they had become cautious strangers, tasting their reaction to each other in this new environment.

6

Teed sensed her uncertainty. 'It's — quite cozy,' she said hesitantly.

'For guests,' he said, 'I have to give up the master bedroom. You will note that it also serves as the living room, dining room and rumpus room. Come here.'

He took her over, opened the door onto a bedroom so tiny that the double bed almost filled it. He said, 'This is my bedroom, and I shall give it up as a dressing room as soon as I get swimming trunks on.'

'Hey, did you mean that about a moonlight swim? I saw the moon coming up but . . . say, isn't that lake cold?'

'Still contains heat from the summer. It's just the air that's cold. I don't suppose you have a swim suit.'

She frowned. 'No. But the undies are nylon. They'll dry fast. We going to have a fire?'

'Sure.'

'Well, go put on your trunks. And then go get in the lake. Those steps I saw when you turned on the light. They go down to the water?'

'Down to a dock. You can dive off it.'

'If I get up the nerve.'

'I'll put you in, if you start to chicken out.'

He changed to shorts in the small bedroom, grinned at her as he went through the living room and out the door. The night wind was frigid. He trotted down the steps, wasted no time getting into the water. It took his breath at first, but it was much warmer than the air. The moon was above the southern horizon, its gold paling to silver blue. Wind ripples lapped against the oil drums on which the dock floated.

When he saw her coming down the steps, he swam in toward the dock. His eyes were used to the moonlight and he saw that she was beautifully constructed, not in a classic way, but in the way made believable only through the efforts of the dreamers who draw the women for gas station calendars. Long smooth limber legs joined sweetly to a torso so short-waisted as to barely escape being out of proportion. Breasts so high, so widely spaced, so firmly heavy that they added a measure of frailty to slim shoulders, to the slenderness of waist.

'Teed, where are you? My t-t-teeth sound like a Spanish dance.'

'Dive in and get it over with.'

'One, t-t-two, th-th-three.' She slanted off

the dock, pale in the moonlight, sliding into the water as sleekly as an otter. She came up, swimming hard and fast. She grabbed his shoulder, panting. 'You cheated me. It's like ice.'

'A sissy, eh? Where'd you learn to dive like that?'

'Water show.'

He remembered his promise just in time to keep from asking the obvious question.

'Hey, it isn't too bad, is it? Race you.'

She got a head start on him. It took a surprisingly long time to catch up with her. They were both breathless. She rolled over to float on her back. She floated high in the water, as all women do, and the soaked nylon was transparent in the bright moonlight.

He felt desire move turgidly within him, quickening the beat of his pulse.

'Teed, do you have anything I can wear after we're through swimming?'

'Jeans and a wool shirt all right? Just take what you want out of the closet to the right of the door as you go in. Haven't you got anything with you?'

'Yes, dammit. But what I've got isn't right for — a camp, as you might well imagine. And I don't want to put the suit back on.'

'Take a fresh shirt from one of the laundry

covers. The others are maybe a little ripe. Ready to quit?'

'Or else take a bite out of my own arm. I've never been so hungry. I'll go first, Teed. You come up when I turn the light off and on again.'

'Modest, eh?' he said.

Her tone turned to ice. 'Let me know if it bothers you. It's a trait I don't get much chance to indulge.'

'Please, Barbara. That's something I would have said to anybody.'

'I'm sorry. Maybe I'm hypersensitive. And I guess that's a luxury too.' Something had gone out of her voice. Some necessary warmth.

'Now you take Albert. He was hypersensitive too. Used to hate to have the pigeons watching him.'

'Fool!' she said, her voice chuckling warm in her throat. She grabbed his shoulders and ducked him strongly. When he came up, she was racing toward the dock, her arms lifting slim and fleet in the moonlight.

When the light blinked he pulled himself up over the edge of the dock and ran shivering up the steps. As he came through the door she tossed a towel to him. She had built a respectable-looking fire, and it was just roaring into life.

'Dry in front of the fire. Look, I found the brandy and the ice and everything, but no mint. You out? You do want stingers?'

'Mint in the bottom cupboard in back. And the right measure is about two and a half to one. How's the fit of those clothes?'

The shoulder seams hung halfway to her elbows. Under the rolled-up jeans she wore a pair of Teed's wool socks. She'd used a length of clothesline as a belt.

'What do you think? Talk about bags tied in the middle.'

He towelled himself, went into the closet and grabbed a twin to her outfit, and shut himself in the bedroom. Her clothes were in there, her purse on top of them. He took five twenties from his wallet and put them in her purse.

By the time he got out she had made the drinks, set up the card table in front of the fire, found a clean sheet to serve as a tablecloth.

'Vegetables nearly thawed,' she said. 'Do you cook the steaks, or do I?'

'I'll do it. How do you like yours?'

'Rare. If you'd taken a minute more, I'd have eaten mine raw.'

Between them they got everything ready and had time for a couple of drinks while the steak sputtered. Barbara said, 'A good swim. I tingle all over.'

Her hair, flattened when she had left the water, had sprung back into damp ringlets. She looked at him with nothing more in her eyes than the warm glow of friendship.

'You're a nice guy, Teed.'

'That's an attempt to get your steak quicker, my friend.'

'You saw through it, didn't you? It just doesn't pay a woman to be subtle any more.'

They ate hugely and with vast concentration. They had a leisurely cigarette, brandy in the coffee, and then they cleaned up.

Afterward the constraint came over them again and he, sensing it, said, 'There's cards around here. Ever play double solitaire?'

'Not since I was a kid.' They played three games. He won the first. She won the next two, her face flushed, her eyes dancing; squealing as they both raced to put a card on one of the ace piles.

'Enough?' he asked.

'I can't stand the excitement. Say, can we watch the fire? I mean with another log on and the lights out?'

'Practically standard operating procedure in a camp, isn't it? Sure.'

She sat in front of the fire, hugging her knees, staring into the flames. He lay on his stomach beside her, his chin on his fist.

'Teed, do you look into the flames and see things? Crazy things?' Her voice was almost a whisper.

'It always makes me feel sort of sad, Barbara. Remote and far away. As though I could look into flames and tell the past and the future.'

'They aren't good things to think about. Pasts and futures. Not good at all.'

He rolled onto his side, reached out and caught her hand. 'Barbara, I . . . '

The dreaminess left her voice. 'It's your choice, of course.'

He let go of her hand quickly. 'What the hell's the use?' he said thickly. 'It's an artificial situation and you can pretend just so long and just so far. Why don't you stay up and watch the fire for a while? I think I'll turn in.'

She stood up quickly. 'I'll get my things out of there.'

She brought out her clothes, purse, overnight bag, put them on the living-room bed. She turned toward him without expression. He rumpled her hair with his big hand, feeling the tender skull-shape under the crisp curl-cap. He bent and kissed her cheek. 'I didn't mean to pop off. Sleep tight.'

'What you said was right, Teed. It is an artificial situation.' She looked at him with an odd dignity, in contrast to the absurd fit of the jeans and shirt. 'We shouldn't have had the pact. We shouldn't have tried to pretend.'

He shrugged. 'Maybe not. But once you start pretending, you're stuck with it, aren't you?'

When he came out of the bathroom she was squatting on her heels by the fire, poking the coals with a twig. She didn't turn as she said, 'Good night, Teed.'

' 'Night, Barbara.'

He shut the door of the tiny bedroom, stripped and slid down between the cool sheets. He swung the window open, hooked it. The night air came through the screen, touched his face with its coolness.

He picked his trousers off the floor, fished out the day's last cigarette, lit it. He lay with his fingers laced behind his head, the cigarette sticking up from the corner of his mouth, and thought about the strangeness of the day, the strangeness of the girl out by the fire.

It's your hundred bucks, he thought. What the hell is wrong with you, Morrow? What do you think she is? Stop thinking of her as some kind of a princess, or as a proper and untouchable young lady from Bryn Mawn. How many others have paid their hundred? One hundred? Five hundred? A thousand?

What were the others like? Puffy little tired businessmen, trying to pretend they didn't pay cash on the line. Wealthy college kids trying to be men of the world. And she's had them all, performing her fundamental female function with all the mechanical joy of a robot with a tin smile. She's a hundred-buck call girl, Morrow, and if you want it, open the door and call it. Then you can take a shower and go to sleep. She's out there squatting by the fire, with her dainty little butt on her dainty little heels and smiling her dainty little smile at a sentimental slob named Morrow who let himself be smarted out of his hundred dollars. Those kittens soon get over any sentimental view of life, Morrow. She's a nail-hard kid. You going to let her spend the next month telling her brassy blonde friends about the guy named Morrow who treated her like a friend of the family?

But, try as he might, he couldn't merge the two images — the image of Barbara the call girl just wouldn't merge with the image of the Barbara who had swum with him, laughed with him, eaten steak with him.

He couldn't call her. He butted the cigarette, punched the pillow and tried to find a position in which he could sleep. Wind rattled the juiceless leaves of autumn. A chipmunk trotted across the roof. He tried to think of Felice, of the danger he was in, of the wet dark look of Raval's eyes. But each time Barbara slid back into his mind.

The door swung slowly open, and she was silhouetted in the doorframe in the red light of the dying fire. The baggy shirt and jeans made her look childlike.

'Teed,' she said in a choked voice, 'Teed, I . . . ' And she stumbled to the bed, to his arms, kneeling beside the bed with her face in the hollow of his throat and shoulder as she wept. He held her, his left arm tight around her shoulders, smoothing her crisp hair with his right hand, making small sounds of comfort as she wept heavily, dully, hopelessly. For a time she vocalised her sobs, as a child will. And then the sobs became dry, thick gasps that came further and further apart.

She straightened up, still kneeling, and knuckled her eyes. 'Sorry, Teed,' she said huskily.

'Everybody has times when being alone is no good.'

'I shouldn't have used you for a wailing wall.'

'Want to talk about it?'

'It isn't important. You just remind me of somebody, Teed. When you walked up to the booth my heart nearly stopped. And all evening. Little habits you have. The way you

110

use your hands, hold your head. You think something is nicely scarred over and then it gets opened up again. And you bleed some more.'

'I'll be a crying towel any time.'

She stood up slowly. 'I wanted to be held. Like a kid, I guess. There's too much night out there. And looking into fires is a sad business at best.'

He reached out and caught her wrist, pulled her toward the bed. She resisted at first, then came to him, slackly. He whipped the covers aside, slid her down beside him, tossed the covers back over them.

Her lips were dead under his. 'I'll stick with the pact, Teed. I mean that.'

'I don't want a production,' he said harshly.

The baggy garments could not disguise the long clean lines of her. He unbuttoned the shirt, starting at the throat. She sat up with numb docility and let him take the shirt off, toss it aside. It lit with a click of buttons against the bare board floor. She started to untie the knot in the length of clothesline. He pushed her hands aside, untied the knot, undid the buttons, pulled the harsh fabric of the dungarees down from the rounded silk of her hips. He tossed them after the shirt.

She lay limp in his arms, his left arm under her head, his right arm around her so that his hand was almost under her body. The fire made dying sounds. The red glow had faded a great deal. He held her tenderly, kissed her eyes, her throat. Whenever he kissed her lips, he seemed to taste resignation, a chronic despair. He brought his left hand around so that his fingertips rested, as though by accident, against the pulse in the side of her throat. Her pulse remained slow, steady, heavy. And after a very long time, when he kissed her eyes again, and then her lips, he felt a tiny quiver of her mouth, felt the pulse increase its tempo. Only then did he bring his right hand around her body, slowly enfold the heaviness of her breast, a globe of warmth, a cup from which honey could be drunk.

As he kissed her again, he felt the stir of her lips, felt, against his palm, the subtle tautening, stiffening.

All at once she stopped breathing. And then she took a vast shuddering breath. Her arms, which had been limp at her sides, slid up and around his neck, and she found his lips with an open, savage hunger.

He was a man who had picked patiently, gingerly, at the stones at the base of a dam. And suddenly the whole structure had collapsed, overwhelming him in the torrent.

She was torrent, and tempest, and whirlwind.

Broken bits of meaningless words glittered in the darkness.

On a dusty shelf in the back of his mind he found a distant childhood memory. They had been a gift — a lot of curiously shaped little wooden bits. The directions were on the box. He had worked at the puzzle until he had grown angry. And suddenly, when he was close to tears, the little wooden parts had fitted together perfectly. You knew at once that all the time they had been made to fit that way. You wondered how you could possibly have gone on that long without recognising the essential and pure perfection of this part going here, and that part going there. It was such locked, perfect precision that it had taken him much longer to tire of that toy than the others that had arrived on the same birthday.

And now, again, here was a co-ordinated rightness, a fitted precision.

He was running up a long flight of black velvet steps. Each step was almost impossibly high, yet he was running with the buoyant fleetness that can be remembered only from dreams. He knew he had to run with perfect cadence. There was no top to the flight of stairs. They went on forever. They went on to the stars and beyond.

And suddenly there was a group of stairs

far steeper than any of the others. In spite of their steepness, he ran even faster — ran up and then out into empty space, into a high, wild, airless place full of the shrillness of a scream.

As in dreams, he did not fall. He floated slowly down to a place where he could again feel the diminuendo of spasmed warmth under his hands, taste the metallic echo of blood on his lip.

After a time she was apart from him. He said, in a slow whisper, 'Oddest damn thing. Was in a school play once. Rehearsed every day for a month. You know, you make me feel as if all I'd ever done is rehearse. And now this was for real.'

'Shut up!' she said tonelessly.

He stared at her. There was just enough light left so that he could see she was on her back, with her right hand, palm upward, resting on her forehead.

'What's the matter?'

'God, God, God,' she said in the same flat, dull tone.

He reached for her and she thrust his hand away.

'Now look! Just what have I done?'

'You couldn't possibly understand.'

'Why don't you try me? Try to tell me, darling.'

'And don't use that sappy, sticky, sentimental tone on me, Teed.'

'You sound like a psycho.'

'OK, you get your explanation. Turn on the light.'

'Why?'

'Just turn it on.'

He sat up, groped for the ceiling-light pull, found it in the dark. He squinted at the harsh impact of the light. She got lithely out of bed, turned and faced him. She stood in an ugly way, feet spraddled, belly outthrust, shoulders slumped. On her face was a hard and bitter expression, and a look of careless violence.

'Take a good look at the stock in trade of a hundred-dollar-whore, my friend.' Even that posture could not make her body ugly. 'Inspect the merchandise.'

'Don't do that to yourself, Barbara. Stop,' he said softly.

Her voice coarsened. 'Poor, poor, poor little Barbara. The delicate, sensitive little thing. Don't make me laugh! Most of the customers want a good look at what they're buying. What's wrong with you? Shy, or something? I've been able to peddle this without fear or favour because it hasn't meant any more to me than a . . . a topcoat. And it has been just as devoid of feeling. It has been like renting a coat. Do you see what I mean?'

'I think I do. You mean it wasn't like selling yourself, because Barbara wasn't actually involved?'

'They buy the trimmings, but they don't buy me. I hide back inside myself and laugh like hell. Once upon a time I got paid for diving into a swimming pool. This isn't half as hard, and the pay is better. But do you see what you've done to me? Now I'm selling too much of myself. Nobody else bought what you just bought, Mr Morrow. Body and soul and emotions and wanting and ... '

'Please, Barbara.'

'I could go on doing this if you hadn't come along. Now I can't go on with it. Maybe it seems like a pretty delicate moral point to you, my friend, but it's important to me. I hate you for it, Teed. And I hate myself worse.'

He lunged quickly, captured her wrist, got the light pull with the other hand. He pulled her roughly back into the bed. She struggled and caught him once across the throat with her nails before he pinned her arms.

'Let — me — go!'

'Stop it! I didn't buy a damn thing, Barbara. Not a thing. I won't give you a cent. Whatever you want to think, just keep remembering that it wasn't a commercial transaction.'

'No matter what you say, whether you pay me or not, you're just another customer.'

His voice was thick. 'Barbara, listen to me. Can't you remember? We've known each other for years. This was a date for a picnic and a moonlight swim. It just got out of control — changed into something else. It could happen to any date.'

'Crap!' she said.

'Have you forgotten old Albert so quickly? And the sleigh ride, and the barn dance?'

'Don't try to help me. Please don't try to help me, Teed,' she said, in an entirely different tone.

Suddenly, unaccountably, his eyes were stinging. He said, 'What a load of guilt for one human being to try to carry, Barbara! You are a crazy, wonderful, damn-fool girl.'

She freed one hand gently. She said, 'Teed, your voice sounds so odd. I don't know . . . ' He tried to turn his head away, but her fingertips brushed his cheek, just under his eye, brushed the dampness.

'Big baby,' she said huskily, tenderly. 'Big baby to bawl over a thing like me.' And then her voice broke and she began to cry again. He held her as he had before. This was a different sort of weeping. After a time she said, 'Help me, Teed. For God's sake, help me.'

His answer was to tighten his arms around her.

When the tears were over, she moved away a bit. 'Got a cigarette?'

'On the floor under your side.'

She found them, gave him one. The match flared briefly and he saw her cheeks go hollow as she took the first drag.

'When they've asked, I've given them a story. A lie every time. No two alike.'

'You don't have to tell me, Barbara.'

'That's where you're wrong. I do. I have to tell the truth to somebody. I guess I've always known that some day I would have to tell the truth to somebody. I went to the right schools, lived the right way. Got engaged to a boy named Roger. A sweet boy, I thought. I told you how you remind me of him, Teed. We were going to be married. I was a virgin. We started sleeping together. It got . . . pretty physical. I mean we were good together. It was in my home town. Baltimore. Roger's boss was a bachelor. We began to see a lot of him. I knew he was a sort of a wolf, but I didn't have to worry. I was Roger's, and we were going to be married and have a zillion kids. One night Roger told me his boss was out of town and we could use his boss's house. I didn't like the idea very much, but he was insistent. We went out there. Roger

118

kept making drinks for me. The whole world got pretty fuzzy. I went to bed with Roger. When morning came, I found out that I was in bed with his boss. Roger had gone home. Roger got a promotion two days later. His boss had made the offer, obviously, and Roger had accepted, prepared the groundwork, dutifully left me there.

'I tried to kill myself. I didn't have enough courage.'

'Or you had too much,' Teed said.

'The worst part was hearing Roger tell me that we could keep on just like we were. I told him what he had turned me into, and what that made of him. He didn't care to be called a pimp. He slapped me. I left town. I didn't care where I went. Maybe I was a little crazy. I came here. A man picked me up. I didn't even care about that. It didn't matter. I made him give me twenty dollars. The next afternoon a woman named Gonzales came to the hotel room. I don't know how she found out. She explained things to me. I didn't want anything to do with her. After she left I went for a walk and the police picked me up. She came to the jail and explained again. So it was either spend ninety days in jail, or do it her way. And that, Mr Morrow, is how I got my start.'

'Roger gave you the name, so you took over the game.'

'I suppose that's it.'

'And all this is just a process of getting even with him, getting even with life.'

'Oh, it's very simple, Teed. I buy nice clothes, live in a nice apartment with an unlisted phone. I'm always honest with myself. I get up in the morning and look into my mirror and say, 'Good morning, you whore'.'

'Maybe I'm a prude. I just don't like the sound of that.'

'And of course I do.'

'Don't get angry. How about your family?'

'The usual thing. They think I'm a model. Isn't that almost standard procedure?'

'What are you going to do now?'

'I . . . I just don't know. I don't know what you've done to me. I feel as if I'd been sick, somehow, ever since Roger. Now I'm getting well. And that makes a problem. I just don't know.'

'All right. I'll rephrase the question. What are you going to do this minute?' he asked, reaching for her.

She moved joyously toward him, her laughter soft in the night. 'Oh, Teed, I can answer that question. I can answer it.'

'We can answer it.'

'Teed, not fierce and . . . desperate, like before. Tender, this time. Slow and tender. Can you pretend tenderness?'

'I don't have to pretend,' he said, his voice thick.

'Can I say a silly thing to you?'

'Of course.'

'Forget, Teed, that the body is shopworn. Just keep remembering that the emotions haven't been used much. They need tenderness. Oh, so badly.'

'That isn't silly. I can understand that.'

'And we must have a new pact. We won't use one word. It's *verboten*, that word. Love. Never say it to me, Teed. Never, never, never, my darling.'

'No love, no pasts, no tomorrows.'

'Just here and now, Teed. Right here and right now I'm your girl. My heart is your heart.'

The red glow of the fire was entirely gone. The wind had died. Far away a car droned through the hills and a dog bayed, sadly, forlornly. The night sky was vast over them, and the dark side of Earth turned slowly toward the sun. For a little time they were able to forget that the only constant in life is the utter loneliness of each individual.

Later, when she whimpered in her sleep he touched her shoulder and, without waking, she made the tiny warm sigh that is the only thing left of a fear that has suddenly gone away.

In the night he shut his fist until his knuckles ached, and thought that maybe one day he would make a trip, call on a man named Roger something.

7

Morning sun was slanting into the small window and Barbara Heddon was shaking him awake.

'Teed! Someone at the door. Wake up, Teed!'

He crawled across her, snatched his trousers off the floor, pulled them on. He shook his head hard, grinned at her. 'Don't get up. I'll chase them away.'

'I think I better get dressed.'

The hard knocking came again, and a man's voice called, 'Open up, Morrow!'

'Coming, coming,' he bellowed angrily.

He flung the door open. The pasty cop named Harry stood there, perennial match stick in his mouth, hat shoved back. Behind him was a gaunt, hard-shouldered, rock-faced man with dull eyes and a gold tooth.

'What do you want?'

'We come with your mail, Morrow,' Harry said. 'See, in the mail you get a warrant. Search warrant. And we're taking you in for a couple questions. I'm Detective Pilcher and this here is Detective Boyd, and that guy getting out of the car with the big black case is named Broznahan and he's from the lab. You alone?'

'There's a lady here. A guest.'

The match slid over to the other corner of his mouth. 'Now aren't you the one! Great entertainer, aren't you?'

'Why the search warrant?'

'We got a hot tip, Morrow. We got a hot tip that you been tipping over the Mayor's wife up here in your camp.' He nudged Boyd. 'Get the joke. Tip. Tipping?'

Broznahan had thick glasses and a thin sharp oversized nose. Teed heard a sound behind him and turned in time to get a glimpse of Barbara, clad only in the wool shirt, scurrying into the bathroom, her clothes over her arm.

Teed stopped blocking the doorway and the three men went in. 'What are you after?' Teed asked.

'Oh,' said Harry Pilcher, 'just a little evidence that Mrs Carboy was here, say Monday night.'

'I thought she was killed Monday night.'

'Gee, you catch on real quick.'

'Am I supposed to be charged with murdering her?'

'Did we say that? We just want a little chat with you, that's all. You know, sit around and chat and giggle and scratch ourselves.'

Broznahan went to work in the kitchen. With his powder and brushes and lens and camera and tape, he was a busy little man.

'Why don't you take this delightful opportunity to put on your city suit, Morrow?' Pilcher asked.

Teed shrugged. He got his clothes from the closet and put them on in the bedroom. Barbara's purse was still there. He took the five twenties back out of it and put them in his wallet. He was back out, completely dressed, a few seconds before Barbara came hesitantly out of the bathroom.

Both the detectives stared at her. Boyd snapped his big fingers. 'Wait! Don't tell me. Hell, you're on Marie Gonzales' list! I see you once in the line-up.'

'You *paying* for it now?' Pilcher asked Teed incredulously.

'Clever of you to figure it out, Sergeant,' Barbara said acidly to Boyd. Her face had hardened and her voice had gone thin and flat.

Boyd sauntered closer to her and fingered her breast roughly. 'You know, I was wondering were those real.'

Barbara neither flinched nor moved away. 'Now you know, Sergeant. So take your hand away.'

'How about a quickie, baby?' Boyd said earnestly.

'Cut it out!' Teed said, anger filling his throat.

Boyd stared at him. 'Hell, your time's up, ain't it?' He turned back to Barbara. 'Right in that room there. Come on. What's the fee?'

'I told you . . . ' Teed said.

'Please, Teed. I can handle this.'

There was a look of warning in Barbara's eyes. She smiled at Boyd. 'Sergeant, I like you. You're so direct and so manly. I'll make you a special price, just because I like you.'

'How much?' Boyd said, reaching for his wallet.

'I like you so much, it will cost you five thousand dollars.'

Boyd froze with his hand on his wallet. Then he whipped his arm around and hit her over the ear with the heel of his hand. She bounced off the wall beside the bathroom door and landed on her hands and knees.

Teed reached Boyd in one step, swinging as he stepped, swinging as Boyd turned blindly into the blow and caught Teed's fist flush on the nose. Teed felt the cartilage and bone go under his knuckles. He chopped hard with his right, followed the reeling man back to the wall, hooked with his left to a belly that felt as hard as a board fence. Boyd doubled and as

126

Teed moved back to measure him for the blow that would knock him down, there was a soft thud against the back of his head. It did not feel like a violent blow, but the vibration shuddered in his brain and turned his knees to water. He felt as though it were taking him forever to turn around. Barbara swept by in the range of his vision, just getting to her feet. There was a dance of steps behind him and another of those soft thuds. This time his legs folded and he went down onto his knees. He waved his arms like a man on a tightrope and got one foot under him again, came back up onto both feet, feeling as though he stood at a dizzy height.

Boyd came toward him, both big fists held low, chin on chest, blood patterning the white shirt. His eyes were squinted almost shut.

'Now, don't mark him! Don't mark him!' a far-off voice yelled.

Boyd hit him under the heart. It was like being hit with a slow sledge. Boyd had swung from close to the floor and the blow lifted both Teed's feet off the floor. He sat on the end of his spine, rolled back and tried to kick feebly at Boyd's knees.

Boyd picked him up and swung toward the wall. Teed flailed with arms that felt as light and ineffectual as those long balloons sold at circuses. Boyd moved in close to him and tucked a massive shoulder under Teed's chin. And with his fists, with slow measured fury, he began to tear Teed's middle apart. He snorted with each blow. Teed could no longer lift his arms. They dangled loosely and his head bobbled on Boyd's shoulder. He tried to grin across the room that seemed full of red mist. Barbara, her face too white, stood flat against the wall. Harry Pilcher stood tapping his palm with a leather sap, his lips pulled back from his teeth. Broznahan stood transfixed, jar in one hand, brush in the other, the light catching his glasses so that his eyes were invisible.

Teed wanted to tell them that Boyd was going to kill him if they didn't stop him. His teeth chattered insanely as his head bobbed on the thick shoulder. Boyd grunted with each blow, twisting his heavy body to get the back muscles into each blow, moving in a slow, almost sexual rhythm. Broznahan, Barbara and Pilcher receded until they were tiny figures, almost too far away to see, and then the red mist drifted across them at the very moment that Boyd's blows stopped hurting entirely.

He came to on the Indian blanket on the living-room bed. In the moment of regaining consciousness, his knees came up hard, as high as he could draw them. It eased the pain in his middle.

Barbara sat beside him. She wiped the sweat from his face with the cool damp washcloth.

'Where — are they?'

'Pilcher is in the bathroom cleaning Boyd up, darling.'

'Could have — taken him. Sapped me, though. Couldn't . . . '

'It was my fault, darling. My fault. I should have known better than get wise with Boyd.'

'He won't — try to force you to . . . '

She smiled without humour. 'Not unless he wants to start talking soprano.'

'Shouldn't — talk hard that way. Jesus, I hurt. Can't get my knees down.'

'Don't try yet. The last thing he did was back up fast and kick you before you could fall.'

'Get — even sometime.'

'Don't think about it now.'

'You — leave. Take my car. Leave it . . . City Hall lot.'

'I'll stay with you and see that you're all right.'

'Please . . . important. Tell Armando Rogale. Lawyer. That'll keep them — from working me over too much. Here's keys.'

She took the keys, concealed them in her hand. She kissed him lightly on the forehead.

'Goodbye, Teed. And thanks.'

She walked quickly and quietly out. He listened and heard the Ford start, heard her give it the gun. He grinned at Pilcher as the man came running angrily out of the bathroom.

'She's used to better — company, Pilcher.'

Pilcher walked over to the bed. 'Oh, how I love them wise! How I love them with a nice big fat chip on the shoulder! Morrow, you're going to be so goddamned eager to tell us you killed Mrs Carboy that you won't be able to get the words out fast enough.'

'And you'll be wondering — how an ex-cop finds a job.'

'Hell, boy! I forgot you're a reformer. I was just thinking of you as a murderer. Forgive me, huh?'

By the time they were ready to leave, Teed could stand up, but he couldn't straighten up. And he couldn't walk without support. He knew, from their attitude, that they hadn't found a thing. Broznahan seemed dis-gruntled.

With Boyd on one side and Pilcher on the other, they walked him out to the car. He had to take one step at a time, and he walked like an old man, unable to lift his heels clear of the ground. They put him in the back seat with a grim, silent Boyd, who held a wet folded towel against his nose.

They drove him into town, drove him to a precinct station in West Deron, took his tie, belt, shoelaces, pocket articles and led him back to a ten-by-ten cell containing two iron bunks, a wall faucet, a pail, a tin cup and a toilet without a seat. He eased himself down onto the bunk and then lay in the only comfortable position he could find, on his side with his knees drawn up. He was almost asleep from exhaustion when Pilcher and a stranger came in. The stranger was in uniform pants and shirt sleeves. His corded forearms were covered with a pelt of red hair.

'He's real stubborn, Harry?' the stranger asked.

'He doesn't know we're trying to help him, Mose. Just hold him for me.'

Mose handled Teed with the same ease with which Teed would have handled a child. He swung him out of the bunk, forced him down onto his knees, facing the bunk. Mose sat on the bunk with Teed's wrists imprisoned in red hands that were like vices.

'Turn it up, Georgie!' Pilcher shouted. A radio began to blast music so loudly that it sounded like a sound truck was right outside the cell.

When the blow fell, the scream tore itself out of Teed's throat before he could think to stop it. He turned his head. Pilcher stood spread-legged behind him, grinning and swinging a regulation billy by the thong. 'Little kidney massage, boy. If I'm careful there won't be any permanent damage. But sometimes I get careless.'

The second blow chopped into the opposite side and this time Teed suppressed the scream.

Mose grinned at him. 'Don't make it tough on yourself, friend.'

Teed let his muscles go slack. Then suddenly he snapped both wrists up, against Mose's thumbs. The instant his hands were free, he lunged forward and drove his right fist into Mose's face. The blow was feeble, glancing, but oddly satisfying. He kicked backward and his heel hit something soft. His laceless shoe fell off. They grabbed him again and the third blow drove him down into darkness.

★ ★ ★

They shook him awake. It was dark. The single cell light was a small bulb behind steel mesh in the cell ceiling. He struck out at them.

'Hey, easy!' Armando said. Teed wanted to roll over onto his face and weep with relief.

'Come on. Get hold of my arm.'

'We better take him to my house,' Powell Dennison said. Teed hadn't recognized him in the gloom.

'Wait a second, before we get him on his feet,' Armando said. 'Teed, here's your stuff from the desk. Powell, get the belt in his pants. I'll fix up his shoes.'

Teed licked dry lips. 'I didn't tell them anything.'

'So we hear,' Armando said. 'How many times they work you over?'

'I don't remember which parts were real and which parts were just dreams.'

'You wore out some stalwart officers of the department, Teed. You even converted Pilcher. Leighton told me that Pilcher refused to touch you again. He said he wasn't going to get in any mess where you had to kill somebody before they'd talk.'

'Are you taking me out of here?'

'Dennison went bail. The charge is assaulting an officer in the performance of his duties.'

'He was trying to . . .'

'Save your strength. I had a talk with the girl.' Armando slipped an arm under his. 'Come on, fella.'

Every step was torture. Every breath he took was like so many knives being forced between his ribs. He leaned heavily on the two of them, the morose turnkey following along behind.

They went slowly up three stairs and the turnkey opened a barred door. He pulled it shut after they went through. There was a short hallway that opened into a large room. Several cops were standing around. Pilcher was there, chewing his match. Leighton stood by the doorway to the street. Everyone watched him.

Pilcher said distinctly, 'These crazy guys. Always falling down a flight of stairs or something. Feel better, Morrow?'

Teed stopped walking. He pulled his arms away from Armando and Powell. He pulled himself erect and the effort dizzied him. Then, planting one foot slowly in front of the other, he walked steadily and slowly and unsupported over toward Pilcher. Pilcher took a step backward, then thought better of it. His eyes were wary.

Teed stopped in front of Pilcher. 'You,' Teed said softly, 'are a sadistic sonofabitch.'

'Now, look!'

'You're a poor policeman and a poor human being.'

'I don't have to take that!'

'Then hit me again, Pilcher. If you don't like the words, hit me again.'

Pilcher looked at the cops, who were watching silently. He laughed nervously. 'What are you going to do with a guy like that?' He turned away, walked quickly through an opposite doorway.

Armando caught Teed before he fell, and they got him out to the car. Teed sat in the back seat. After two blocks he began to cry, sobbing aloud.

'Easy, boy,' Armando said.

He stopped before they reached the Dennison house. Jake and Marcia stood wide-eyed and silent in the hall as they brought him in and started up the stairs with him.

'Phone Dr Schaeffer, Marcia, please,' Powell said.

He asked to be permitted to stop and rest at the landing. Jake squeezed by them and went on up the stairs. A bedroom light clicked on. Teed could not see the bed, but he could see it in his mind. Deep and soft and white and eternal.

After a few moments he felt as though he could make it the rest of the way. The bed lamp glowed on the white pillows. Jake had turned the bed down and she stood silently in the shadows. Her father said a low word to her and she left. Armando and Powell helped him undress.

The doctor seemed to arrive almost immediately. He was a brisk man with a military mustache. Armando and Powell stood back in the shadows as the doctor prodded softly, expertly. 'Hurt? Now breathe. Again. This hurt?'

'Should he go to a hospital, Doctor?' Powell asked in the soft voice used in a room of the sick.

'I . . . don't think so. Who — what happened to this man?'

'Would you be willing to testify that he was beaten?' Armando asked.

'I'm quite busy. Testimony means appearing in court. Delays.'

'Would you sign a statement?'

The doctor was silent for a long moment. 'Really, it's hard to be certain about a thing like this.'

'What damage is there?'

'I wouldn't care to say just yet. I'll want samples. Urine, stool. There'll be some bleeding. Superficial kidney damage, I would say. Of course, a severe fall would . . . '

'A fall where he bounced a few dozen times?' Armando asked acidly.

Schaeffer straightened his shoulders. 'I am fresh out of lances, sir, and I have no quarrel with windmills. I've seen this sort of work before. My work is to heal.'

'And never stick your neck out,' Armando said.

'Please, Mr Rogale,' Powell Dennison said.

Alcohol was a touch of coolness on Teed's arm. The needle was a point of fire in the cool patch. 'I'll stop by in the morning,' Schaeffer said. 'He'll sleep until then. I'll decide in the morning whether we should take him in for X-rays. There's no definite rib fracture. Maybe a crack or two. This man has a very powerful body. I suspect he may snap back quite rapidly.'

The doctor left. Powell went down with him. Teed heard their low voices on the stairs and in the lower hallway.

Armando said, 'I think you'll stay sick quite a while, Teed. So sick they can't haul you in again.'

'If they started on me again I . . . I don't know.'

'You've made a friend, Teed. Herb Leighton. Sorry I couldn't get you out quicker. They hadn't booked you. Said at headquarters you weren't in custody. Leighton had a job finding out which precinct you were in.'

Armando's voice went on and became a buzzing sound that made no sense. Teed hauled himself back up out of the enclosing darkness. His speech sounded drunken. 'I missed that last part, Armando.'

'I said that the Heddon woman was a little unpopular with the boys right now. They didn't like the way she ran out. So she's laying low for a while. I found her a place. If they try to bring that assault charge to trial, she's willing to testify on your behalf. What the hell did you do to her? Give her religion? She must know that if she sticks her neck out for you, they'll give her a train ride to Dannemora.'

'Don't . . . let her do it,' Teed said. His voice sounded as though it were echoing through a tunnel.

'Hey, boy. Those ginches are expendable. She takes her own risks.'

Teed could hold his eyelids open no longer. He was vaguely conscious of the light going out, of soft footsteps, of the closing of the room door. The pain of each breath lost sharpness. It was no longer pain. It was a deep blue light that glowed with each inhalation. It was apart from him.

Chairs were drawn close to the bed. They all sat there, their knees touching the bed, all their shoulders touching. They all sat in the dark and watched him under the blue light. Each time the light glowed, he could see their faces, the shadowed eyes.

'Who is this man?' they chanted softly.

'Who is this man who was once a boy?'

Voice of his father, 'He is my son. He was my son.'

Voice of the sister long dead, 'My brother.'

Voice of the lovely Ronnie, 'My lover. Father of the bastard child which, because of two hundred dollars and ten degrading minutes, was never born.'

And voice of Felice, coldly, 'He is my murderer. So I am closer than the others.' Chant of the black-haired daughter, 'He is my soul.' Incantation of Powell, 'He is the son I might have had.'

Whispered voice of Barbara, 'He is my shame.'

And back in the echoing caverns of his mind, in the trackless paths which lead to no open space, Teed Morrow raised his head and screamed until the neck cords stood like cables. 'Who am I?' he screamed. And the answer was a shot that made no sound, sent him tumbling over and over, down and down into darkness, between walls of slate.

8

'How are we this morning?' Dr Schaeffer said. After-effects of the injection were like clouds, his mind like an aircraft that flew through them, alternating bright lucidity with the almost overpowering desire to sink back into sleep. His tongue felt as though it had been split, packed with cotton, resewed.

'From neck to knees, Doctor, I feel like a dull toothache. The rest of me is fine.'

'You're like a rainbow. I can pick out six distinct colours. Hungry?'

'Definitely.'

'You're on a bland diet. Milk toast, soft-boiled eggs. Yesterday's fever is gone. You're subnormal right now. X-ray plates show nothing.'

'Wait a minute. Yesterday's fever? What's today?'

'Friday, Mr Morrow.'

'Wasn't I brought here last night?'

'No. Wednesday night. You've lost a day. Can't you remember any of it?'

Teed frowned. 'A few bits and pieces. Can I get up?'

'This afternoon, if you feel like it. You can

get dressed tomorrow. Avoid bending over, picking up anything heavy. There's some abdominal-muscle damage. Not much, but enough to be careful about. Stop in my office Monday morning.'

The doctor left. Teed could sense his own weakness. He shut his fists, and could not shut them tightly. After a time he heard steps on the stairs, the clink of dishes. Marcia came in with food on a tray table.

'Good morning, nurse,' Teed said.

She was crisp, quick, smilingly polite. She bent over him to pull the pillows up. She smelled of soap and some floral perfume. She looked as though she had been scrubbed with a harsh brush until she glowed. Viking woman.

'Did I make the papers?' he asked.

'I'll get them for you. The *Times* played it down. The *Banner News* convicted you, on the front page, of drunken assault, lechery, obstructing justice. They slyly hinted that you killed Mrs Carboy, but Mr Rogale told Daddy that some legal eagle had gone over the story before it was printed, so there's nothing actionable.'

'I guess I've got a little dirty linen to hang on the public clothesline.'

Her lips tightened a bit. 'That's your affair, Teed. Not mine.'

'Marcia, are you as prim inside as you look outside?'

'I'll get the papers now,' she said.

He went over the Thursday papers and the Friday morning *Banner News* carefully. The only important thing was to determine if Dennison had been hurt by this. He flushed as he read the editorial in the *Banner News*.

'Mr Powell Dennison is, we understand, highly regarded in the field of municipal administration. However, it appears to us that Mr Dennison's background has been more theoretical than practical. Many intelligent men who perform a valid function in institutions of higher education find themselves somewhat at a loss when it comes to the give and take of the everyday world.

'It is no slur on Mr Dennison's standing, professionally, to raise certain questions about his capability in the matter of employing personnel. He had known and worked with Mr Teed Morrow in the past. So rather than select his assistant from among the many capable men who know the ins and outs of Deron politics and procedures, Mr Dennison went far afield to bring Mr Morrow here from some position or other in Pennsylvania. Personal loyalty is fine. When it is given more emphasis than effective administration, it becomes dubious.

'We hold no grief for Mr Teed Morrow. Perhaps he performs his assigned work efficiently. That is for Mr Dennison to say. But Mr Morrow has come here and in six months he has apparently grown to believe that because of his position, he stands apart from ordinary moral standards, and feels himself to be beyond the touch of duly constituted law and order. It is up to the courts to unravel the more intriguing aspects of Mr Morrow's personal habits. We can only conjecture about the known facts. One — Mrs Mark Carboy's automobile was found in front of Mr Morrow's apartment on the morning following her death. Two — When Officers Boyd and Pilcher went to Mr Morrow's rented camp at West Canada Lake to question him regarding Mrs Carboy's car, they found Mr Morrow in the company of a notorious woman whose name has appeared on the police blotter on three separate occasions. Three — When Officers Boyd and Pilcher attempted to question Mr Morrow, he assaulted Sergeant Boyd and broke his nose. It was necessary to use force to bring Mr Morrow into custody.

'We do not feel that Mr Morrow's actions are what we should expect of any public servant.

'We humbly suggest to Mr Dennison that

he request Mr Morrow's resignation and that Mr Morrow be replaced by one of the capable citizens of this city.

'Should Mr Dennison refuse to request the resignation, we can only assume that it is, in effect, an approval of Mr Morrow's personal habits and attitude toward authority. If this be the case, the *Banner News* wishes once more to reaffirm its policy stated at the time the Mayor-City Manager form of government appeared as Option Three on the ballot. If your house needs cleaning, the thing to do is get out the rags and the soap and the bucket and get down on your knees and do it yourself.'

★ ★ ★

Teed crumpled the paper and threw it aside. He lay back and stared rigidly at the ceiling. The editorial was damning. It contained enough facts to make every honest and decent citizen of the city lose confidence in Dennison. And confidence was what Powell Dennison was going to need at the time he made public his findings to date.

When Powell came home, Teed had made his decision. Powell pulled a chair over to the bed. 'Did you read the editorial in the *Banner News*, Powell?'

'A very clever and thorough job. But that's their job, Teed. To make us look just as black as they possibly can.'

'I handed it to them on a platter, Powell.'

The big man frowned. 'I don't see that. You had nothing to do with the car being left there. And you know that I've never tried to control your personal life, Teed.'

Teed propped himself up on one elbow. 'The nicer you are about it, the more you make me feel like a heel. Damn it, I want you to drop me over the side. I insist on it. I'm resigning, as of right now.'

Powell shut his eyes for long seconds, opened them slowly. 'Job too tough for you?'

'You know better than that.'

'Is it the beating you took, Teed?'

'No. It's the fact that I've lied to you. I lied to you because I was doing something I knew wasn't smart, and I didn't want to stop because Felice Carboy was good in bed. Oh, not wonderful, you know. Just pleasantly competent.'

Powell smiled. 'That isn't exactly news, Teed.'

'When did you know?'

'One Sunday the girls and I drove out. Her car was there. The two of you were swimming. I walked back to the car and told

145

the girls you weren't around. So we drove on.'

'Why didn't you collar me and tell me I was being a fool?'

'It's a man's privilege, Teed, to be a fool. And a woman's privilege too. I suppose that taking that other woman out there was Rogale's idea. An attempt to cover up?'

'All right. Do you know that Felice Carboy was killed at my camp? Do you know that I brought her body back and left it where it was found? Two specialists came out and took care of her very adequately.'

Powell said softly, 'That isn't very good, is it?'

'All they need is just a little more evidence, real or manufactured, Powell, and I'm in the soup.'

'If you resigned, Teed, they would stop hunting for evidence. Is that what you're trying to say?'

'That wasn't my reason. It is a reason, but not mine.'

'It's a risk I don't want you to take, Teed. And there's a way out of it. That was last Monday night, wasn't it?' He got up quickly and went to the head of the stairs. 'Girls!' he called. 'Come up here a minute.' He went back into the room. 'Jake is home from school for lunch.'

The girls came in, smiling at first, then

146

sobering as they sensed the tension in the room.

'Think of Monday night. What happened? Phone calls? I don't remember getting any. We had no visitors, did we?'

Teed saw where it was heading. 'I can't let you do this.'

'Be quiet. Girls?'

Jake said, 'It was a real quiet evening. I had homework piled up. You remember anything, Marse?'

'As far as I can remember, no one came and no one called,' Marcia said firmly.

'Now understand this, girls, and remember it, please,' Powell said. 'I worked in my study until nine. I told you I had some things to go over with Teed, things I'd forgotten. I drove the car up to West Canada Lake and we worked so late that I stayed overnight, as I told you I might when I left, and I came back in the morning.'

'But, Daddy,' Jake said, 'why do you have to . . .'

Powell caught her hand. 'Some people are trying to frame Teed, honey, for something he didn't do. I'm willing to perjure myself and ask you two to lie for me in order to make it impossible for them to frame him easily. You don't have to agree. But if you do agree, you can't change your mind later.'

Jake looked at Teed with shining eyes. 'Of course, Daddy. We'll do it, won't we, Marse?'

Marcia nodded, as though it were of little importance.

★　★　★

Rogale came in mid-afternoon and Marcia woke Teed up from his nap. Armando looked tired. He put his briefcase on the floor beside the bed.

'Your attorney reports, Teed. Jeez, what a day!'

'How does it look?'

'Well, somebody got to our ex-mayor, Judge Kennelty, with the idea that as long as we have the Heddon girl on ice, they'd be damn fools to press this Boyd question. The Deputy Chief, Wally Wetzelle, told me over the phone that the charge was being withdrawn. I picked up Dennison's bail receipt and went and got his dough back. The opposition sort of faded away. Like swinging at a baseball and hitting a powder puff. I can't say it makes me happy.'

'Why not?'

'You only drop one attack when you think of a better one. On a hunch I got hold of a contact I have in the D.A.'s office. Apparently as far as Trim is concerned, the Carboy kill is still 'person or persons unknown'. And my contact said that Wetzelle, in charge of the case, has cut the working crew down to one guy, a vague, unworldly cop named Dinst who would have trouble finding the pay phone in a phone booth. It looks like there is going to be another unsolved murder in the files of our fair city. So my uneasy feeling grows stronger.'

'What's the policy?'

'Watchful waiting. What the hell else? Unless you people want to leap to the attack. Got enough yet?'

'Enough to get a return of grand-jury indictments against Kennelty, Koalwitz, Carboy, Joseph Lantana and three members of the Common Council. Conspiracy to defraud the public.'

'I see what you mean,' Armando said, nodding, 'enough for a big stink, some indictments that won't turn into convictions. A stink that will slowly blow away and leave the same guys in the driver's seat, eh?'

'Nothing to touch Lonnie Raval, Armando.'

'Or his two upstanding young lieutenants, Windy Weiss and Tony Stratter. I can see how previous you'd be, popping it now. Raval would just dump the ones you got the goods on and replace them out of stock. Are you getting any closer?'

'Maybe we were, and didn't know it, Armando. Maybe Felice was the key for the lock. I wish I knew what she was going to tell. Think Carboy knows?'

'He probably does. And if he does, Teed, he'll gabble just like Harpo Marx. He's like the other ones that jump when Raval snaps his fingers. Stupid and shrewd. A hell of a combination. It makes me think of the TV programmes during the investigation. You could see them there, the fat-cat smarties. They sweated a little and they squirmed a little, but when it was over they hopped planes and got the hell out of there. It was the dime-a-dozen politicians that were left standing by the wringer, wondering how they got caught. And not one of them with the guts, even after being caught, to come right out and name names, trace connections, point the finger at the fat cats. No. Always waiting and hoping for a new appeal, waiting until the heat was off so they could go nuzzling back to the fat cats, saying, 'See? I didn't tell a thing. Now get my muzzle back in the trough. Loyal guys like me should be rewarded'.' Rogale jumped up and walked over to the window, setting his heels down hard. 'They've got something in mind,' he muttered. 'I wish I could guess what it is.'

After he had gone, Teed put on the slippers

and robe that had been brought over from his apartment. He went downstairs slowly, holding onto the railing. By the time he reached the downstairs hall, he was sweating and trembling with weakness. The house was empty. He saw the car full of kids slow down in front, saw Jake jump out, wave and yell at the car, come running up the steps. She wore a flaring wool skirt of Chinese red, a white cardigan.

'Hey!' she said. 'You supposed to be up?'

'They told me I could. Now I'm beginning to wonder.'

'I think you'd better sit down before you fall down, Teed. Sit on the couch. Here, I'll put the pillows down at this end.'

When she had him fixed, she sat on the couch, down by his feet. She looked at him and the flush crept up from her throat, suffused her cheeks. She looked away quickly. 'I'm sorry about last Sunday night, Teed. I got kind of creepy.'

'Not too many of your birthdays ago, I upended you and paddled you. With one to grow on. Maybe you were getting even, Jake.'

Her eyes were bold, suddenly. 'It worked, didn't it?'

'What worked?'

'That one to grow on. I grew, didn't I?' She lifted her chin and squared her shoulders.

Teed looked quickly away from the white cardigan.

'Jake, you mustn't get . . . crazy and impossible ideas.'

'About us, Teed? Oh, I know what you think. What you and Daddy and Marse think. That I'm a fool kid with a crush on an older man. You can go right on thinking it. It won't hurt any. Because I know you're wrong. I love you and I'll always love you. It isn't kid stuff. I'm eighteen, Teed.'

'Barely eighteen and a high-school senior.'

'Look at me, Teed. Stop looking across the room. I'm old enough to have children. Your children. I want your children, Teed.'

'You've *got* to stop all this.'

'I've figured it all out, Teed. When I'm thirty, you'll be forty-three. When I'm thirty-six, you'll be forty-nine. And we're right for each other. Couldn't you tell when I kissed you Sunday night?'

He looked at her blazing eyes, at her intentness. He said slowly, 'I didn't feel any more or any less than I would have felt kissing any eighteen-year-old girl-child. It was very refreshing.'

'You're trying to hurt me, trying to drive me away. You can't, Teed. I'll never give up. Never!'

'You'll meet a guy tomorrow, maybe.'

'In school?' she said contemptuously. 'One of *those*! Some pimply creep who just wants to get you out in a car and put cold hands on you.' She shuddered violently.

'Look, can we just drop the subject?'

She made one of her lightning changes of mood, became very demure. Eyes downcast. 'Of course, darling. If it tires you to talk about it.'

'Don't call me darling!'

'Not if you don't like it, dear.'

'Give me strength,' he muttered. They heard Marcia come in the back door, dump bundles on the kitchen table. She came in, her cheeks pinked by the crisp wind of early November.

'Smells almost like snow out,' Marcia said. She stared at them. 'Why are you looking angry, Teed, and why is Jake looking like a whipped pup?'

Jake stood with great dignity. 'I'm afraid, my dear elder sister, that is none of your affair.' She stalked out.

'Well, fawncy that!' Marcia said, one eyebrow tilted high. 'Say, are you going to eat at the table with us tonight?'

'I think so.'

'Are you feeling better?'

'Just a little shaky. A lot of the pain is gone.'

'Was Jake being silly again?'

'Thoroughly. I suppose I ought to be flattered. It just makes me feel like somebody's grandpop. I hoped those newspaper articles would expose my feet of clay.'

'Oh, no. She told us that after you and she were married, there'd be no reason for that sort of nonsense.'

'I give up.'

'And that's exactly what she expects you to do, Teed.'

'Look, you're her sister. Do you have any influence?'

'Not the least bit. She calls me the 'glacial' type. She says that I can't possibly hope to understand an undying passion.'

'Could you, Marcia?' he asked, wondering why he always felt it necessary to needle the girl.

She bit her lip. Without answering she turned and went out with her lithe stride, hips so firm as to almost be called chunky, swinging the tweed skirt, treading as lightly and surely as an Indian, or a Viking maiden. In her was none of Jake's gawky grace. Marcia moved all of a piece. Teed had seen other girls who moved that way. The water skiers at Cypress Gardens. The equestrians with the circus.

Powell came home a bit later and decided that a bland drink for Teed would be in

154

accord with his bland diet. After dinner Teed reported Armando's comments.

Powell said, 'He's right when he says we can't move in on Raval yet. Maybe we'll never be able to. That Weiss is the bag man, the pickup man. Tony Stratter handles the pay-offs. Everything is cash. When and where and how Raval steps in for his cut is a deep mystery. That's our choice, Teed. To wait and hope we can get some more while we strengthen the data we already have, or whether we pop it fast. I suspect Raval would like to have us step up to the plate right now.'

'Which is the best argument for waiting that I can think of,' Teed said, smothering a convulsive yawn.

'I forgot how this would tire you, Teed. Better go to bed.'

'I'm OK. Just sleepy. I'll be to work by Monday.'

'Don't rush it. There's plenty of time.'

'I wonder just how much time there is,' Teed said. He said good night to Powell and the girls and went up to bed. He was lost in a warm mist of sleepiness. Consciousness left him with almost the same speed that the room fell into darkness when he pulled the bed-lamp chain.

* * *

The dream has taste and colour and texture. A woman-dream of astonishing vividness, of clinging warmth, of heavy scent. He struggled up through the soft strands of sleep to the awareness of the warmth against him.

'What in the . . . '

A hand like ice closed his lips. 'Hush, Teed,' she whispered.

He pulled her hand away and whispered, 'Dammit, Jake! What do you think you're doing?'

She was shivering violently and her breath was coming fast. She pulled his arms around her, burrowed closer against his chest, her hair tickling his nostrils. His hand rested on a silky sheerness, on the trembling warmth underneath it.

'Oh, Teed, I love you so!'

'My God, you've drenched yourself with perfume!'

She shook with silent laughter. 'Did I use too much?' she whispered. 'I couldn't see in the dark. And I couldn't turn on the light. It's nearly three. They're asleep. I took one of Marcia's nightgowns, too. I don't have any like this.'

He wormed his imprisoned arm out from under her, rolled onto his back, folded his arms across his chest. 'Jake, you go back to your own bed,' he whispered.

'Love me, Teed. It will be all right. We'll be married, Teed.'

'By God, I'm not going to touch you. Go away. Get out of here.'

She rammed her head up into his neck, an arm across his body. 'You can't win, Teed. Even if you don't, I'll say you did. So see? You'll have the name anyway, so you might as well have the game.'

'What do you think a man's made of? I don't love you. Even if I did, this would be a damn fool operation. Go back to your own bed, dammit.'

'I've got enough love for both of us, my darling.'

'OK. You've got enough love for both of us. Let's discuss it in the morning.'

'Please stop talking, darling.' She climbed up over his shoulder, found his lips with hers, her arms sliding around his neck. The scent was like a cloud around them.

He pushed her away. He heard movement and thought she was leaving.

'What are you doing?' he whispered.

'Just a moment, darling. I'm getting rid of this thing. I don't want to get it all crumpled up.'

'Put it back on. At once!'

'Too late. Ah, much too late,' she whispered, sliding back against him, pressing hard against him, round warmth against him. Her breathing was quick and shallow, her hands chill, her heart racing so hard that he felt its soft thud against his arm. He knew that she was frightened, seriously frightened, but beyond threats, beyond repulse. His will told him to get out his side of the big bed, walk over to the windows, get a cigarette from the bureau. But the sweetness and the warmth had stirred him. Even as he resolved to leave her, he turned toward her, sliding his right arm under her, finding her lips, finding, under his fingertips, the long incredible silken slope of her back. And as he searched her mouth, he felt the stiffness of fear in her body, as his hand swept across her body he felt the shrinking, the virgin reluctance, the shock at the impact of maleness.

It was enough, and just barely enough, to break the spell. He pushed her away and moved back so that they no longer touched.

'I'm not afraid, Teed,' she said in a barely audible whisper, and he knew that she had realized what had made him stop.

'Unless you're out of this room in thirty seconds, Jake, I'm going to turn the lights on, get dressed, and leave this house.'

'You can't. You're not ... well enough. Teed, please.'

'I never meant anything more than I mean

that, Jake. And I'm right. You would have hated me, afterward.'

'I could never hate you.'

'Get dressed, Jake.'

He watched. The room was so dark that she was nothing but a pale shadow. He heard the silky rustle. Her perfume grew strong again as she leaned over the bed. Her lips were like a child's lips. They touched his cheek, slid lightly to his mouth.

'Good night, Teed.'

'Good night, Jake. This never happened. We dreamed it, Jake.'

'It never happened, my darling.'

The door latch clicked and then clicked again as it shut. There was a faint creak of a floorboard in the hall. Silence. Just the perfume left, more faint than before. He clenched his fist and struck hard at his upraised thigh. Little girl playing games with a woman's body. Little girl with sophistication borrowed from cheap movies, philosophy from the confession magazines, glamour from the pendulous bosom of television.

He struck his thigh again and then grinned into the darkness. Not such a stupid little girl, maybe. She'd certainly left him wound up like a four-dollar watch. But better than the other way. Better than hearing her harsh intake of breath at the first stab of the incredible, unexpected pain. Better than listening to the brave smothering of child tears. Better than the feeling of unthinking brutality and shame that would be his. He composed himself for sleep, knowing that it would come reluctantly, if at all.

9

When he went downstairs dressed, at ten, Powell had gone to the office, Marcia was marketing. It was Saturday and Jake was home. In blue jeans and fuzzy yellow sweat shirt, she bustled around the kitchen, getting his breakfast.

She talked too gaily, her voice pitched too high. He noticed that she was pale and there were blue shadows under her eyes.

She served the bacon and eggs and toast and coffee, then sat at the table across from him, head tilted, cheek resting on her clasped hands, elbows on the table.

'I suppose every person makes a mistake once in a while, Teed.'

'Standard practice.'

'Thank you for saving me from making my mistake.'

'You're welcome. You cured now?'

'What do you mean?'

'You've got over me, I hope.'

'Oh, goodness, no! I lay awake and I realized that all I was doing was cheating us. Our first time won't be like that, Teed. Not sneaking and hiding and whispering in the dark. No, it will be in a big hotel. Maybe in Havana. With a little patio off the room. And we'll have all the time there is. Just think! All the time there is.'

'When is this alarming sequence going to take place?'

She frowned seriously. 'Now I figure it this way, Teed. I haven't told Daddy, but I've been changing some of those silly pre-college courses to practical things. Home Economics. A course about babies.'

'Do they tell you where they come from?'

'Now, don't be childish, Teed. This is my senior year. I'll be out in June. I think I can break it gently to Daddy, about no more school, I mean. My birthday comes on June twenty-sixth. School will be out then. This job you and Daddy are doing ought to be quiet by then. And if we get married on my birthday, you'll only have one date to remember instead of two. Men are so backward about remembering dates. And they say Havana isn't hot at all in the summer. Cooler than Florida, they say.'

'You stayed awake and organized my future, did you?'

'I don't want a big wedding. A really big wedding. Do you?'

'This is pretty sudden, you know.'

'And sex is important, of course, but not all

important. Having kindred interests is a big part of it. Our backgrounds, in general, are the same. Of course, I'll take courses after I'm married, so I won't be *too* stupid for you.'

'Honey, just let me eat my eggs, will you?'

She beamed at him. 'That sounds so nice and married, Teed. 'Honey, just let me eat my eggs, will you?' Oh, Teed!'

'Look!'

'And you should realize that marrying a younger woman will help keep you young. You won't get stuffy so fast. I'll catch up, and then we'll both get stuffy together. I want babies right away, so I'll be a grandma before I'm forty.'

She got up and said, 'Now, darling, I'll let you have your breakfast in peace so you can think it over. You don't have to tell me today, or anything.'

'Thank you for the grace period,' he said hollowly.

After breakfast, and after Marcia came back, he repacked the bag that had been brought from his apartment.

'You're not leaving!' Jake cried.

'I can take care of myself now, thanks. Just a little stiff. Not sore a bit any more. I'll take a cab down to the Hall, stop in and tell Powell and drive my car back to the apartment. I can't tell you how much I appreciate all you've done.'

He left in a storm of objections and solicitous advice. He lowered himself gingerly into the back seat of the taxi and waved at the two girls standing on the porch, Jake a half-head taller than the blonde Marcia.

★ ★ ★

Most of the Hall was on a five-day week, but there was enough traffic so that Teed sensed the intensity of the interest in him. Girls left their desks quickly to walk with overcasual step into the hall, just to be certain of seeing him. The Teed Morrow of a few days back would have felt a certain amount of wry amusement, would have enjoyed the sensation of playing a part in a drama that touched him lightly if at all. Now he could not capture the necessary emotional remoteness. It was even an effort to keep from hurrying his steps to get out of range of the avid curiosity as quickly as possible.

As he went up the stairs a vast, billowing woman from the City Engineer's office came down. She had always favored him with a mincing smile. She looked at him and through him, and sniffed audibly as they passed. City employees seem to develop a seventh sense. Catastrophe casts an invisible aura over its victims before it strikes. You must sense that aura and move carefully away to avoid sharing in a common disaster. Teed knew that this new attitude would also take in Powell Dennison. Co-operation would be much more difficult to obtain. Necessary records would remain stubbornly in the files. Even the switchboard would be slow and uncertain.

The little people on the city payroll had waited and watched, not quite certain whether or not the move toward new efficiency and economy would bear fruit, would affect them and their jobs. Now, mysteriously, word had gone out that it would all come to nothing, and so there was no more reason for caution. Now was the time to back away and say, 'I knew it was a farce from the beginning.'

Even the sallow face of Miss Anderson showed the effects of the new attitude. The lines were etched a bit more deeply around her mouth, and she flung the typewriter carriage back with a clattering smash at the end of each line.

It was an old story to Dennison and Teed. They had felt it in the German city when it appeared for a time that higher command would force a revision of policy on the matter of employing known ex-Nazis. And, in the end when Dennison had won his point, the attitude had changed mysteriously even before the statement of policy had been received.

Teed walked into Powell's office. Powell leaned back in his chair. 'Teed, you walk like you were carrying a pie plate between your knees. Should you be up and around?'

'I kissed the girls goodbye, Powell, I'm going back to a bachelor existence.'

'Jake give you a bad time?' Powell said, with his slow warm smile.

Teed flushed. 'Not bad enough to drive me out of the house. How'd you get a daughter as stubborn as that?'

'Her mother gave me just as much trouble.'

'Powell, do you feel the change of attitude around here?'

'It changed Thursday, Teed. The word went out, I guess. They're wrong, you know. It's going to be a hell of a shock to most of them.'

'Makes you wonder what the hole card is, doesn't it?'

'Not when we've got aces showing, Teed. I finished that assessment survey. It shows enough so that when the *Times* publishes the results, nothing can stand in the way of the city hiring independent experts to come in here and revise the whole tax setup.'

'I'm going to take it easy over the weekend, Powell, but that's no reason I can't work on something at the apartment. What can you give me?'

'Sure you want to? OK. Take this file. Don't let it get out of your hands. It shows tax sales of unimproved property. A whole bunch of building lots just inside the south edge of town. And here's a transcript of property sales in the same area. And a map. Seems that one L. L. Weiss has picked up a lot of land out that way.'

'Windy? Raval's boy?'

'Right. And Sandscone, over at the Chamber of Commerce, advises me that he talked with Devlin, of the Board of Education, and Devlin said that the area in question is the logical place for the new high school. Devlin expects the bond issue to be approved.'

'Oh, fine!' Teed said. 'Weiss is dummy for Raval. Raval picks up the land, pressures Devlin to locate the high school there, pressures the Common Council to approve the bond issue, sells the land at a fat profit and then has one of his own companies put in the low bid on construction, knowing that he can get the co-operation of the inspectors and cut enough corners in construction so that the profit is fat.'

'In a way,' Powell said slowly, 'Raval is telling us, by going ahead with this thing, that he doesn't think we can hurt him. He isn't even doing us the courtesy of battening down his hatches until the storm is over. Take the folder, Teed, and see if you can write up the facts in such a way that Ritchie Seward can carry the ball with a series on it when we're ready to fire.'

Teed took the manila folder and stood up. 'I'll be on my way. Thanks, Powell.'

Powell looked a little uncomfortable. 'I suppose I ought to tell you this. I had a little session with the men who put up our war fund. They don't like this recent development. They wanted to get back more control of the purse strings. I talked them out of it.'

'This time.'

'Right. Well . . . take it easy.'

'Thanks for telling me, Powell. Is Carboy back on the job?'

'Not yet. The funeral was Thursday. He left the hospital Thursday morning, and now he's at his home. They expect him to be back in the office Monday.'

'Funny it should hit him so hard, Powell. Hell, he must have realized that Felice wasn't . . . I don't know how to say it.'

*　★　*

168

He found his car in the City Hall lot. He hunted for the keys and found them in the ash tray. When Barbara had fled from Boyd and Pilcher she must have known that she was making enemies who could do her harm. He had been too dazed to realize at the time what he was asking her to do. The wind was raw. He closed the windows and turned on the heater.

Mrs Kidder was at the desk. She seemed more shy than usual as she handed him his mail. He tried to revive the jokes between them, but there was no response in her. He realized that her attitude toward him had been changed by recent events, and he was annoyed that it should bother him so much.

'Mrs Kidder?'

'Yes, Mr Morrow.'

'Did you ever hear that about believing half what you see and nothing of what you read?'

'Yes, I've heard that, Mr Morrow.'

'You give me the impression that you're critical of me.'

She met his glance for longer than ever before and then looked away. 'When people pay their rent and don't annoy the other tenants, Mr Morrow, it's not my place to be critical.'

He shrugged and turned away, anger thick

in his throat. As he walked across the central park toward his apartment, he leafed through the mail. Bills and ads. Except the last one. A personal letter. Feminine handwriting. Grey stationery with a white border.

He stopped outside his door to read it.

Dear Teed,

It is hard to write this sort of a letter without it sounding like something to be spoken in a throbbing voice with violins in the background. Actually it is a letter of thanks. I feel as though I have been ill for a long time, and now I am beginning to convalesce. I thought that what I had done to myself had been entirely my own business, but now I have begun to paraphrase Mr Donne and think about no woman being an island unto herself. You were the shock I needed, Teed, and when Mr Rogale tells me that there is nothing I need to stay here for, I shall be off to distant places to see if I can put myself back together, bit by bit. I know that it is certainly far too late for me to become, in any respect, a junior leaguer, but at least I can become honest with myself. Give my very best to Albert and the pigeons.

Your Barbara

There was, of course, no return address. He unlocked the door and went in. He sat down and picked up the phone book, found Armando Rogale's home number. He put his hand on the phone, then shrugged and tossed the book on the shelf of the phone table. Seeing her again would not help her, or him. To stir other persons, cause them to examine their own motivations, open them to self-doubt, is a responsibility that should not be lightly assumed. In stripping Barbara of her tough defences, he had realized how fragile were his own. He was quite certain that she would not want to see him. Once the catalyst has caused the chemical reaction, its function is over. The reaction, once started, is self-sustaining. He knew that Barbara would not dramatize herself or her decision. As a woman and a human being she had set out to punish herself for some real or imagined lack. The punishment was over. The organism had survived. It was altered, irrevocably, but it had survived.

He was still sitting at the alcove phone table, his back to the door, when he heard it swing open, felt the coolness on the back of his neck.

He turned quickly, chair legs sliding on the hardwood floor of the alcove. Mark Carboy leaned his back against the door, slamming it shut. He was hatless, and his hands were deep in the slash pockets of his dark overcoat. His eyes were puffed, reddened, and completely wild. Carboy was a big-bellied man with a long hard-boned face. The flesh appeared to have slid from his face, gathered in loose folds that overlapped his collar. It was a face which, in photographs, seemed full of a steel-eyed resolution, and in life looked oddly broken, as though something deep within the man had snapped long ago.

'Mr Mayor, I . . . I'm glad to see you,' Teed said inanely.

'Get on your feet, Morrow,' the man whispered.

Teed stood up slowly. The revolver was grotesquely huge. It was the biggest revolver Teed had ever seen. The absurdly large eye of the muzzle wavered in a slow circle, a small circle with Teed's belt buckle as the centre point.

'What do you want?'

'I'm going to kill you,' Carboy said. Sweat stood out on his forehead. He reached his left hand over and strained to pull back the massive hammer. The cylinder revolved with an oiled click.

'What for? Dammit, what for?' Teed cried, knowing that he sounded abused and petulant, almost childish.

The muzzle lifted until it pointed at the centre of his chest. Teed knew that, through shock and surprise, he had lost his opportunity. At that range, the revolver would blow the entire centre of his chest out through his backbone.

Carboy stuck his tongue out of the corner of his mouth, looking like a man trying to thread a needle. Teed heard a hard roaring in his ears and his vision misted until the only thing that stood out with painful clarity was the eye of the muzzle, the blade sight above it.

The second went by. 'Do it, then!' Teed said. 'What the hell are you waiting for?'

The trembling started in Carboy's knees, spread upwards until his whole body shook like that of a person in a chill. His teeth began to chatter. Teed saw the arm lower slowly until the muzzle pointed at the floor. Carboy stood with his eyes shut, his lips bluish.

Teed turned mechanically, woodenly, and marched to a chair and sat down. He leaned his head back and closed his eyes and concentrated on taking deep breaths.

Carboy walked in and sat on the couch. He laid the gun beside him on a cushion. They stared at each other and Teed felt the odd camaraderie of two men who have closely avoided a disaster.

'Close,' Teed breathed. 'God, was that close.'

'I thought I could do it. I was so sure I could do it.'

'Drink, Mayor?'

'Please.'

Teed walked to the small kitchen on knees that threatened to bend the wrong way. He broke cubes out of the tray, splashed generous measures of bourbon onto the cubes, added water to each, carried the glasses back in. Carboy's glass chittered against his teeth as he drank deeply. Teed picked up the gun, swung the cylinder out, pulled the trigger. The hammer snapped down with a rat-trap noise. He shoved the cylinder back in and handed the gun to Carboy. Carboy took it gingerly and shoved it into his pocket.

'Hate guns,' he said. 'Always have.'

'Where did you get a cannon like that?'

'My father brought it back from Silver City in the eighties. Forty-four Colt, I think it is. God, Morrow, I feel as though I'd been bled white.'

'You,' Teed said, 'are not alone. What was the idea, anyway?'

'Because you killed my wife, Morrow. Revenge, I guess.'

'But I didn't kill her!'

Carboy stared at him without particular interest. 'I know that.'

'Would you mind going over that slowly, Mayor?'

'I don't understand it very well myself. If I could cling to the belief that you killed her, Morrow, stick with that belief right up to the point of killing you, then the act of killing you would fix that belief in my mind. Maybe the idea was that once you were dead you couldn't deny it strongly enough to shake my belief.'

'Isn't that pretty metaphysical, Mayor?'

'The other choice, Morrow, is less pretty. If you didn't do it, then it was done by the orders of the people who put me where I am. And that isn't an easy thing to fit your mind around. Men take your courage and your honesty and your self-respect, and then, almost as an afterthought, they kill your wife because she still has those qualities, in part, that you have lost somewhere along the line.'

'And that's what was going through your mind when you were on the verge of blowing me in half?'

'That was the argument for doing it, Morrow. The argument against it is that I can't kill. Even to regain self-respect.'

'Did she mean that much to you?'

Carboy chuckled. It was an unpleasant

sound. 'Felice? She enjoyed being the first lady of the city. She wasn't going to give that up, you know. I was the pimp. Ugly word, isn't it? She bought our prestige in her own way and between us we split the gains. And they like that. They knew that Felice made me easier to control. Any man who is thoroughly sick of himself is easy to push around. Felice made it profitable, too. I backed Raval's ventures up with public oratory, and each public bump and grind I did fattened the kitty.'

'Then why did you take it so hard, Mark?'

'Because I killed her, of course. Sound a little irrational, don't I? Felice decided that Dennison is going to win. She wanted to gamble on it. She wanted to trade immunity for me for information that would assure Dennison's winning. I was afraid, Morrow. We fought it out until the small hours of Monday morning. And she won. So I told Raval what information she was going to give you. I wanted her stopped. I didn't think Dennison would lend himself to such a trade. So Raval . . . stopped her. You see, if I could keep forcing myself to believe that you killed her, Morrow, then I would be guiltless.'

Teed leaned forward. 'What was the information, Mark? Tell me.'

Carboy shook his head, almost sadly. 'I

won't tell you. It is something I have, maybe the only weapon I have left, and I shall use it as I see fit.'

'Tell me one thing. Is it conclusive? Will it hurt Raval?'

Carboy grunted to his feet. 'It will very likely kill him, Mr Morrow.'

He walked heavily to the door and Teed followed him. At the door, Carboy turned. His eyes were clouded.

'You know, I have been thinking, wondering, just when and where my life changed. It is an odd thing when a man can't remember the exact moment a choice was made. Possibly the choice is never clear-cut. I have been thinking a great deal.'

'The moralists talk about right and wrong, Mark.'

'It isn't that simple. A man enters public life and he tells himself that he will do good. He will be effective and the people will benefit. It is idealism of a respectable variety. And then he discovers that he must make certain compromises in order to achieve good. Like a man who builds a house. To afford the roof, he must order cheaper windows. To afford a fireplace, he must skimp the foundation. The house no longer satisfies him as much as it did, but he tells himself that without the short cuts there would be no house at all.

'But in public life, each compromise makes the next compromise easier, and each move toward good makes the next move more difficult. It is a miserable equation to live with. Yet the man goes on, and he tells himself that if you take the total good, and subtract the total evil, the net result is good. He drifts along, clutching the illusion, until one day he adds it up and he discovers that evil outbalances good. And he never knows the precise point where the balance changed, nor does he know which specific compromise was the wrong one.'

He drew himself up for a moment, and in that moment looked as noble as the retouched election photographs. 'I think slowly, Morrow. I am not quick in my mind. But I do not believe that I am stupid, or that I am consciously evil.'

'I do not believe that either, Mark,' Teed said softly.

'It is time to change the balance of the scales.' Carboy left. Teed stood at the window and watched the black Buick drive away, Carboy huddled in the back seat.

10

The moment Carboy had been driven away in the city sedan, Teed got on the phone. Powell had left the office and was not yet home. He phoned police headquarters, found that Captain Leighton was not on duty, was given Leighton's home phone number.

A child answered and Teed heard him call his father.

'Captain Leighton, this is Teed Morrow.'

'What's on your mind? Going to confess?'

'I want to thank you for helping Rogale find where I was.'

'It was worth it to watch you give Pilcher the works by the desk there. What gives? You got some new murders on your mind?'

'This may be for the wild geese. I don't know. I just had a visit from Mayor Carboy, here at my apartment. This call goes through the switchboard here at the apartments. I wonder if you could come over, understanding that it may be nothing.'

'Most of my life has been spent tracking down nothing. Give me a half hour.'

Leighton arrived in twenty minutes in his rusty black suit looking, with hollow chest, stooped thin shoulders, like a sleepy scavenger bird.

He interposed no questions as Teed told him of the visit.

'And that crack about balancing the scales, Morrow. You think he's gone off with that cannon and a fixed idea of making holes in somebody?'

'I can't think of anything else he would have meant.'

'Mark Carboy has always gone around being dramatic. He's an expert sufferer, Morrow.'

'Maybe this is the one time when he's been pushed beyond the edge.'

'It would surprise the hell out of me, frankly. Long as I'm here, Morrow, I want to ask you something. I heard a rumour yesterday. Heard they're taking the clamps off you because there's a good chance of fitting them onto your boss. I don't know the method. Anything in his past that he wouldn't want dredged up?'

'Absolutely nothing, Captain. You are always hearing about people's lives being open books. In this case, it happens to fit.'

'Either of those daughters of his ever been in a bad jam?'

'I'm sure I would have heard of it if they had. Jake is just a kid. Marcia is a pretty prim sort of girl. Quiet.'

'Sometimes those quiet ones will give you a real surprise. Anyway, it was just a rumour, and it sort of fits with the way they turned off the heat under you.'

'They had no case.'

'Don't kid yourself. They could bring in ten witnesses who would swear to seeing you strangle her in the lobby of the Hotel Deron at high noon, and three guys to testify that you made them help you carry the body out to the dump. But figure it this way. All they can do through you is discredit Dennison. That isn't enough. There are still too many decent people in town behind him, and his reputation in Albany is good enough so that he might bring the Attorney General down on the city with enough ammunition this time to make a difference, no matter what happens to you, even if they managed to fry you at dawn. Dennison is the better target. Muzzling him would change the picture a lot more definitely than ruining you.'

'What will you do about Mayor Carboy?'

'Before I left the house I got hold of one of the few guys I can trust on the force and told him to get on the Mayor's tail and stay there.'

'I didn't tell you anything over the phone.'

'You sounded shaky enough so that it seemed like a good idea.'

'Do you have any idea, Captain, what it was that his wife was planning to tell me?'

'If I had a *good* idea, I'd either be dead or be Chief of Police.'

'You sound as though you might have a hunch.'

'I do. Luke Koalwitz has used the edge of his tongue on Lonnie Raval more than seldom. That is something that just isn't done. But the axe never falls. Commissioner Koalwitz trots around, fat, smug and happy. Men have been killed in this town for less. The word is that Koalwitz gets more than his fair cut of the gravy. It spells one thing to me, Morrow, and I've been thinking about it a long time. Lonnie and Luke grew up in the same neighborhood. I think something happened, maybe a long time ago, maybe just a few years ago. Luke Koalwitz has some kind of evidence on Lonnie that could really put him on the spot. Not a local spot. Maybe a federal spot. He's got it hidden away somewhere and it is his immunity. Luke is a bragging sort of man. He and Felice Carboy got chummy well over a year ago. Do you see how it figures?'

'Yes, I do.'

The phone rang. Teed got it, turned and said, 'For you, Captain.'

Leighton grunted several times into the

phone, then hung up. 'That was my boy. Carboy went home, went right through the house and drove away in that Pontiac convertible. My boy lost him.'

After Leighton had left, Teed went out for a late lunch, came back and stretched out on his bed. He meant to take a short nap before going over the folder he had brought from Dennison's office.

The harsh recurrent jangle of the phone awoke him. It was dark. The daytime sleep had left an evil taste in his mouth. He felt sour and discouraged and dull.

He snapped on a floor lamp at the end of the couch, went into the alcove and snatched up the phone.

'Yes?'

'Teed, is that you? Have you just come in? I've been calling and calling.'

'Hello, Marcia. What's up?'

'Teed, Jake is with you, isn't she?' She seemed upset.

'Jake? No. I haven't seen her all day. I must have been too sound asleep to hear the phone before. What time is it? My watch has stopped.'

'A few minutes after midnight, Teed. I'm . . . worried, so worried. This isn't like her. She's never thoughtless.'

'Where's Powell?'

'Out looking for her, with the car. I've been calling her friends. Teed, could you come over? Please?'

'Of course. As soon as I can.'

He stripped off his clothes, stepped into the shower. He turned it slowly from warm to cold, letting the shock awaken him completely. All of the bruises had turned to an ugly dirty yellow, a few of the more severe ones blotched with purple.

He dressed quickly, paused in the hall, took his topcoat from a hanger and shouldered into it. The night had turned cold, and his breath was visible. He did not want to think, as yet, of what might have happened to Jake.

From Rogale's uncertainty, and from the rumour that Leighton had heard, it seemed entirely possible that Raval's people had picked her up. And yet even Raval shouldn't wish to take that sort of risk. Kidnapping, and it could he nothing else, was a federal offence.

He had to use the defrosters to remove the mist from the windshield as he drove across town to the Dennison house. The porch lights and all the downstairs lights were on. He parked in front and hurried up the steps.

Marcia opened the door before he could knock. Her face looked oddly shrunken. 'I saw you drive up, Teed. It was silly to have

184

you come over. I'm sorry.'

'Then she's all right?'

'I'm sure she's all right. She'll turn up. You better go back to bed, Teed.'

He pushed by her, pulling the door shut behind him. 'What goes on here? Is Powell back?'

'Not yet.'

'I'll wait until he comes back.' He walked into the living room, sat down without taking his coat off. He took out his cigarettes and Marcia came over with a table lighter, took a cigarette, lit his and hers. He watched her. Her hand trembled.

'Have you informed the police?'

'And checked the hospitals. Teed, you'd better go home.'

'Dammit, I'm not a stranger. This is close to being the only home I have.'

She would not look at him. 'Don't ask questions, Teed. Just go.'

He stood up impatiently and took hold of her shoulders. 'Look at me! What happened since you called me?'

Marcia made her eyes too bland. 'Nothing happened.'

Teed shook her so roughly that her head wobbled loosely on her neck and her eyes went out of focus. 'Don't lie to me! Tell me what happened.'

'I can't tell you.'

'Then someone came or someone called. Who was it? What did they say? What did they want?'

'I won't tell you, Teed. You can't make me tell you.'

He released her, sat down. 'You'll tell your father.'

'When he comes, I'll tell him.'

She sat stiffly across the room from him. She had changed in a way that he could not identify until he noticed that she no longer looked controlled, enigmatic. There was a cold, steady anger in her grey eyes.

They did not speak. She was the first to hear Powell's heavy footsteps on the back porch. She hurried into the kitchen, through the dining room, and swung the door shut.

Teed pushed it open. Powell was slowly unbuttoning his coat. He looked ten years older. 'I . . . couldn't find her,' he said. 'Hello, Teed. Good of you to rally 'round.'

'Daddy, I want to talk to you alone.'

He grasped her arm. 'Do you know something that . . . '

'Alone,' she said firmly.

He stared at Teed, and in that moment Teed felt himself to be an outsider. Teed nodded and left the room, let the door swing shut behind him. He walked into the living room. Powell's heavy voice was a low vibration in the back of the house.

And then Marcia's voice rose in anger so shrill that Teed could almost distinguish the words, Powell's voice roared out, drowning hers. Then he called, 'Teed! Come here!'

Teed hurried out to the kitchen. Marcia sat at the table, her face cradled on her arm, her shoulders shaking. Teed looked at Powell Dennison standing, feet planted strongly, his face wearing the most terrible expression Teed had ever seen on a human face.

'This concerns you too, Teed, even though Marcia claims it doesn't.'

Marcia lifted a tear-burned face. 'You'll let them . . . '

'Be still!' Powell roared. Teed had never heard him speak to either daughter in that tone of voice.

'Before you arrived, Teed, and after she had called you, Marcia received a phone call from Jacqueline. My youngest daughter reports that she is not being held against her will, and we must make no more attempts to find her. We must tell the police that she is safe. She says that she will not return home until I have complied with a certain request. Someone will come here within the next hour to make the request. Marcia seems disturbed that I will not permit myself to be bullied in this fashion.'

'How did she sound, Marcia?' Teed asked.

'Frightened. Dreadfully frightened. She said that Daddy *had* to do whatever he was asked.'

'I wouldn't think anything in the world could frighten Jake,' Powell said softly, wonderingly. He walked out of the kitchen. A few moments later they heard the heavy slam of the study doors.

Marcia said, 'You've got to make him do whatever they want, Teed. You've *got* to.'

Teed sat down across from her. 'He's a stubborn man.'

'But not a heartless man. Nothing is more important than Jake.'

'You've got to understand him better, Marcia. He's never been bought. That's what they're trying to do. Buy him.'

'Then it would be stupid pride to refuse. Pride valued higher than . . . my sister. And you want to back him up, don't you?'

'No. I do not want to back him up. But I do know that it's his decision to make.'

'I don't even see how there's a decision, Teed. I don't see how he can . . . even hesitate . . . not knowing where she is or what . . . they're doing to her.'

'When did you miss her?'

'After the dinner dishes were done, she said

she was going down to the corner to pick up a magazine that was supposed to be in yesterday. She never came back. The street is dark . . . she never even got to the store.'

'What was she wearing?'

'Jeans, a red-and-white-striped basque shirt, a short polo coat and a white scarf. Go talk to him, Teed. Make him see what he might be doing to her.'

He stood up slowly. 'I'll try it.'

When he knocked at the study door, Powell told him to come in. Powell sat at the desk, his elbows on the green blotter, his face in his hands. The desk light glared on the stacks of papers, left his head in darkness.

'It's a pretty foul way to try to get at you, sir.'

Powell's voice was remote. 'Now that it has happened, I know that I have been expecting it for some time. Children, they say, are hostages to fortune.'

'Don't you think you'd better do whatever they ask?'

'I am two people, Teed. I am a father. I am also a public servant. In my role as a father I cannot avoid doing whatever they ask. In my official position, I cannot be intimidated. It's an odd feeling to feel yourself being torn in half.'

'This is more important than the job, Powell.'

'Too many people have found too many things more important than their jobs.'

'That smacks of fanaticism.'

'Before I make up my mind, I shall listen to the request. If it is something that I can repudiate later, I shall agree. If it leaves me no opening, I shall call their bluff. They can't really mean to harm her.'

'How can you be sure of that? These aren't human beings, Powell. These are animals we're dealing with.'

'They won't dare harm her. I must believe that.'

'And if they do? What if they do?'

'I can't think of that.'

'If they harm her, you will lose both daughters.'

'And where do you stand, Teed?'

Teed did not raise his eyes from Dennison's strong white fist which rested on the green blotter in the full glare of the light. 'If they harm her, I shall not think the same of you again. I'm sorry. That's the way it is.'

'Is there no decency in the world?' Powell asked, as though he were pleading.

'Now I think you're dramatizing yourself. At least call off the police, Powell, and we'll see who'll come and what the request will be.'

Powell phoned obediently. Teed sat in the study and thought of Jake, of the absurd heaviness of the perfume in the night, of her vividness, so unlike Marcia, of the long sweet slant of back with the small, taut, clever muscles webbed under the milk and silk of her skin, of the way her breath had fluttered in her throat as hands like ice grasped hard in panic and need.

While Powell phoned, Marcia came into the study. She braced sturdy haunches against the desk edge, her arms folded across her breasts, shoulders hunched. He reached up and found her hand and it clasped his tightly.

She said softly, 'You think the world is such a safe place, and then . . . '

'I know. We go around taking too much for granted. You know, Marse, in Germany they told me how it was in the thirties. A knock on the door in the middle of the night. A knock with a pistol butt. And no one to appeal to. No one at all. No court that wasn't a rubber stamp for the bully boys. I used to wonder how I'd react in that sort of environment.'

She squeezed his hand. 'I think I'd compromise until there was nothing left of me, Teed, just out of fear.'

'I heard that word before today. Compromise. Marse, I don't think you would. I think you're strong. You'd fight.'

'Marse. That's Jake's nickname for me. You've never used it before. Teed, we've got to get her away from them. Somehow. Even if we have to . . . '

'You can't force your father to do what you want.'

'Maybe there's something you can do, Teed, that they would want just as much as anything he could do.'

'I work for him.'

'There's a time to forget loyalty.' She took her hand away.

He stood up, facing her. 'We have to wait and find out.'

She didn't answer. He walked out into the living room, suddenly noticing that he still wore his topcoat. He took it off, threw it toward a chair. He stretched experimentally and found that most of the soreness was gone. The sleep had left him feeling fit, resilient.

Powell had long since completed the call. He sat in the dark hall. Marcia walked into the living room. She sat on the arm of Teed's chair and he gave her a cigarette.

'You've changed, Teed,' she said softly.

'How?'

'I've always resented you. This work . . . it has been such an amusing jolly game for you, and so desperately serious to Daddy. I don't mean that I thought you were some kind of wise guy, but I always thought you were laughing at us, somewhere inside. That you felt in some small way superior to Daddy just because he *could* be so . . . well, dedicated. I guess that's the word. And it seemed to me that you liked the impression you made too well.'

'Have I improved?' he asked lightly.

'I think, for the first time, Teed, that you've really begun to fight. I think you're involved now — that you're committing more than just hours of work.'

'I didn't know that I was being judged, Marcia.'

'Now don't get defensive again. I think it is better if we can be friends, Teed.'

'We are.'

'Why doesn't the person come? I'm babbling.'

A car motor stopped in front of the house. A tyre yelped against the kerb. An expensive car door chunked shut and steel-capped heels clacked toward the porch.

11

There was nothing sinister about his attitude. He had the aplomb of an invited guest. 'I'm Weiss,' he said, smilingly. 'Commonly known as Windy. I'll leave the coat here on the chair if it's O.K.'

'Of course,' Powell said.

Weiss was a trim-bodied man with the crisp balance of a boxer. His pale grey suit was cleverly cut to minimise the shortness of his neck. His round head sat squarely on his shoulders. Sparse blond hair was combed straight back. A thin blond moustache helped give him the look of a prosperous young real estate broker. The only remaining signs of his one-time trade were the white-line scars in his brows, thickness of lips, convexity of upper eyelids, hoarse faraway voice.

Weiss walked confidently into the living room. He extended cigarettes with an unspoken question, lit one for himself with a crisp click of his lighter, sat down and pulled a grey trouser leg up a bit as he crossed his legs.

He exhaled and smiled at them. His smile flashed quickly and disappeared at once, without ever changing the expression of the light blue eyes.

Marcia and Powell sat on the couch, facing him. Teed leaned against the mantel, hands in his pockets.

'Your daughter, Mr Dennison, is a very gutsy little lady.'

'Say what you came to say,' Powell said heavily.

'Now don't go into the heavy act, folks. This is a little business conference. Your daughter came to have a talk with us. She's pretty worried about Morrow, here. Seems he has himself in a jam. She's anxious to have him cleared, you know. She thinks a lot of him.'

'You people won't get away with this,' Powell said.

'Get away with what? I don't understand you, Mr Dennison. Your daughter isn't being restrained. She can come home any time. She just doesn't want to. Not until she gets a promise that Morrow here will be left alone. And we can't see our way clear to give that promise until you do us a little favour, Mr Dennison.'

'Resign, I suppose,' Powell said.

'We don't want you to resign. You're doing good work for Deron, Mr Dennison. We're all in back of you. We just think you get a little too eager sometimes. You know. We think you ought to stick to getting the City Hall running efficiently.'

'What do you expect me to do?'

Weiss took two folded sheets of paper out of his pocket. He got up quickly and took them over and handed them to Powell, returned to his chair. He said, 'We want you to copy those in your own handwriting and date them a month ago like it says, and sign them. That's all. It's very simple.' Powell read them quickly. His face did not change expression. He handed them to Teed.

The first one was to Mayor Carboy.

Dear Mark,

In our talk yesterday you told me the basis on which things could be worked out. I have thought it over, and the amount does not seem satisfactory. Please tell the proper person that I feel it should be half as much again. The mode of handling it is satisfactory, and seems safe. You must understand the delicacy of my position, and also understand that I must be free to accomplish certain things to justify this position, though I am quite willing to check in advance as you suggest. Furthermore, I suggest that if F. is to be used, she should be given sealed envelopes for transmittal to M.

The second letter was to Judge Kennelty, and was dated three days after the first letter.

Dear Judge,
Mark has indicated approval of my suggestions, though I am still a bit dubious about F. in spite of his reassurances as to her dependability. M. can be trusted implicitly, and he shall give her the list you mentioned so that you can determine which projects should be dropped. As I told Mark, it is necessary that there should be some record of accomplishment and some of your group will have to be hurt, though I will, of course, leave it up to you to determine which ones.

Teed could easily see the diabolical cleverness of the scheme. Once the letters had been written, there was no longer anything to fear from Dennison. He would be permitted to continue in his job, but if, at any time, he attempted to clean out the Raval group, the letters would be made public. They would show clearly that Dennison had been receiving a rake-off, that Felice Carboy had been the courier, that Morrow, in meeting Felice, had received money and instructions, had sent back Dennison's communications through Felice.

And, in implicating the woman who could not deny her part in it, it made an inference of motive.

Weiss said softly, 'And don't think that you can memorise the letters, write copies, and repudiate them. We've explained to your daughter, Dennison, that unless she denies any knowledge of all this, friend Morrow will still be clobbered.'

'We can tell her that you sold her a bill of goods,' Teed said. 'There's no case against me.'

The flashing smile came and went. Weiss dug in his pocket again and pulled out a three-by-five glossy print. 'We showed her this, Morrow. She damn near passed out.'

Teed took the picture. It was like looking into a nightmare. He sat propped against the wall by the bathroom door, chin on his chest, bottle beside him, the print so clear that he could read the label on the bottle. In the lower left corner of the print, inches from his naked foot, was the swollen horror of Felice's dead face.

'Why didn't you use it before?' he asked, and his voice did not sound like his own.

'A thing like that, it makes the court

wonder who took the picture. Besides, you're the small fry, Morrow. We were just fiddling around, trying to get a lever to use on Dennison here. You know what I figure? Everybody has a button. On some people it's obvious, and it has got a sign on it that says money. But no matter what it says, the button is there if you can find it. It just took longer than usual, Mr Dennison, to find out how to make you jump through the hoop.'

'And you had to kill Felice Carboy anyway,' Teed said.

Weiss gave him a quick look. 'She was getting a little big for her panties. If that's what you mean.'

'Why take this picture if Seward was already tipped off?'

Weiss shrugged. 'Just in case he believed you and tried to cover for you. You did good, Morrow. Everybody got a hell of a shock when she turned up in the dump. You can keep that print if you want it. Keep it under your pillow at night.'

'You expect me to copy out those letters and sign them?' Powell asked.

Weiss's eyebrows shot up. 'What the hell else can you do?'

'And if I refuse?'

Weiss laughed. 'Man, you can't refuse. That kid of yours is nuts about Morrow. If we told her to lay down in front of a truck to help Morrow, she'd do it.' His voice hardened. 'Anything we tell her to do, she'll do. Get it?'

Teed glanced at Marcia. Her face was grey and there was a sheen on her forehead and her upper lip. She looked on the verge of being ill.

'He'll do it,' Marcia whispered.

'I don't want to have to draw pictures for you people,' Weiss said. 'I don't want to have to act like a hard guy. But if you don't play, that kid may get pretty ashamed. So ashamed she won't ever want to come home. We can slip a few studio prints of her into that high school. Kids go for that kind of art work, Mr Dennison.' Weiss' tongue flicked quickly across his lower lip.

Weiss leaned forward. 'And we'll give you a break. You get stubborn and we'll bring you a few prints to show you what we mean. Understand, nobody will be forcing her. If you don't break down then, we'll bring you some action shots, and if you still got a stone head, we'll send her on the road and by then she'll be goddam glad to go and if you ever trace her she'll tell you to go to hell because by then she won't be any kid any more, and you can start wondering when we'll find a way to make this other girl of yours volunteer.' He began to spit out the words, with a spray of spittle. 'You stonehead Christers amuse the hell out of me. You think the law is God sitting on a big bench. Wake up. In this town, we're the law. And we're getting bigger and stronger and tougher and smarter every year. We're expanding, Dennison. We're buying into more legit stuff all the time. And no stonehead like you can stop us. If you want to, you can toss that pretty kid of yours to every hunky with two bucks in his pocket, but it won't slow us down. Now make up your mind and make it up fast and stop acting like this was a big tragedy. This is a business deal. Write those out and she'll be home in half an hour.'

Weiss leaned back and took a handkerchief out of his pocket, wiped his lips.

Powell leaned forward. He stared at the floor between his feet and his clenched fists were on his knees. His head had a palsied tremble. He stood up, his face blank.

'Give me the letters, Teed,' he said. He took them and walked into the study. In the silence they heard the rustle of paper, and then the scuff of his pen as he began to write in his bold distinctive hand.

Weiss said, 'Token resistance. Isn't that what they call it?'

'You're a filthy sonofabitch,' Teed said softly.

Weiss lit another cigarette. 'There's a lady present, Morrow. Are you a lady, sugar?'

Marcia said, 'He'll resign, you know. He won't keep on with the job.'

'We got a guy to put in when he quits, sugar.'

Marcia stared at him, intensely curious. 'What can turn a human being into a thing like you, Mr Weiss?'

Surprisingly, Weiss flushed. 'I'm no different than a million other guys. The only friend you got in this world, sugar, is money. No hard feelings. Your sister'll be home safe and sound in a little bit. I'll take the car over to the Ca . . . over to where she is and bring her right back. Give her a pill and put her to bed and she'll be fine in the morning.'

Powell came out with the letters. He seemed remote. There was no more anger in him. Weiss glanced briefly at the letters, folded them and tucked them in his pocket.

'OK, folks. Thanks, Mr Dennison.'

'You're welcome,' Powell said dully. Teed looked at Powell, and it seemed a hand closed suddenly on his heart. This was the shape of defeat. This was the smell of resignation. Powell even picked up Weiss' coat and held it for him as the man shrugged into it, hitching the collar into place. Weiss grinned as he buttoned his coat.

'Don't take it hard,' Weiss said. 'We'll all get together one of these days and figure out a programme. No reason why we can't all work together.'

'No reason at all,' Powell said.

'No reason why you should live on peanuts, Dennison. Lonnie is pretty generous when things go right.'

'I'll be glad to talk with him,' Powell said.

They went into the hall with him, to the front door. Marcia stood back several feet, one hand reaching up to hold the railing.

Weiss went out onto the porch, turned and gave his flashing, meaningless smile. The big car at the kerb, behind Teed's, picked up high lights from the street lamps.

As Weiss turned back to go down the steps, a deepthroated, booming explosion smashed the night into fragments. The explosion had come from the end of the porch, to the right of the door.

Weiss reacted as though someone had caught him in the shoulder with the full-arm swing of a maul. He smashed sideway through the railing, turning in the air, diving out onto the narrow lawn. Teed turned and saw the bulky figure that clung to the railing at the right end of the porch. It dropped lightly to the grass below and ran silently across the yard.

It stood over Weiss and fired again. The impact made the body appear to leap up off the grass before it settled back. The dark figure turned and in the slant of a distant street lamp, Teed saw the long, heavy-boned face of Mayor Carboy. He turned and walked briskly off. Not fleeing. Not frightened. It was the firm tread of a man who has set himself a complicated mission and is anxious to complete it.

Powell put out a slow hand and supported himself against the doorframe. Marcia had not moved. Her expression was that of a person attempting to identify a distant, puzzling sound. Teed ran lightly down the steps, knelt beside the body.

A raw, plaintive, nasal female voice came through the darkness. 'George! I say that was shots! Why don't you call the police or something? George!'

The man's irritated mumble sounded in the background and a door shut.

Teed sat on his heels beside the body. He touched the arm tentatively and then wiped his hands on his thighs. Enough night vision came to him to make his stomach turn heavily, to bring a sour taste to his throat. The second shot, apparently, had caught Weiss at the nape of his stubby neck. The head was all but severed. This was the end, then, of the tight-moving body, the balanced precision, the husky-hoarse fighter's voice.

Powell spoke softly. 'The police will come. I think those people are going to call.'

'What do you want me to do?'

'Get those letters. The inside jacket pocket, Teed. I'll call Raval and tell him he can have the letters.'

'And say that Carboy walked up and shot Weiss? Who do you think we can sell that to?'

'Get the letters, Teed.'

Teed put his hands under the body, flipped it over, withdrawing his hands quickly. He parted the coat, opened the jacket. He reached in, felt wetness and felt metal, cool against warmth, against fading warmth. He took the slim automatic out of the holster, pulling against the spring, wiped it flat against the grass and put it into his side pocket. He wiped his fingertips on the grass and felt for the letters. They were undamaged. Powell had gone into the house. The street, at two-something on a Monday morning, was dark and silent. A street light two blocks away turned from red to green, a patient methodical robot controlling traffic that was not there.

Teed grasped Weiss' ankles and backed across the lawn, across the sidewalk, to the sedan that Weiss had come in. The coat turned back under the shoulders and the head rested on the coat, lolling loosely over the irregularities in the yard. The loose arms rode with elbows out, hands above the head, palms upward.

Teed opened the back door of the sedan on the curb side. He pulled Weiss in as far as he could, hurried around the car, opened the back door on the other side, reached through and grasped the ankles again, pulled him all the way in. The dome light did not go out until both doors were shut. He leaned against the sedan for a moment, his knees trembling. He bent and looked through the front window. The street light touched the keys, hanging from the ignition.

The porch light went on and Marcia came out, looking out toward the two cars. He went to her. 'Get back in the house. Get the lights off. I put him in his car.'

Powell was hunched over the phone. He said in a low voice, 'But I tell you we have the letters.' He listened, then looked up at Teed with a helpless expression.

Teed picked the phone out of his unresisting hand. 'Who is this?' he asked.

'This is Miss Trowbridge, Mr Raval's secretary,' the sleepy irritated voice said. 'And I can't make head or tail of what . . . '

'This is Morrow. I've met you. The time

Lonnie zeroed in on your head with the golf ball. I've got to talk to him, Alice.'

'He doesn't like to be . . . '

'This is important. Wake him up, dammit!'

He heard her yawn. 'Hold the phone, then. I don't know anything about any letters.'

Teed leaned against the wall and waited. He fished a cigarette out of his pack. Marcia came over with a lighter. He saw her wince and followed the direction of her glance. His right hand was blood-smeared, with bits of grass clinging to the stains. But her hand didn't tremble as she held the light for him.

'Who the hell is this? Morrow? What do you . . . '

'Look, Raval. Just let me talk. Weiss made Dennison a proposition tonight. Don't act like you never heard of it.'

'I haven't heard of it. Keep talking.'

'Dennison agreed. He did what Weiss asked him to do. Now he wants the other end of the bargain kept, Raval.'

'So that's up to Weiss. I got nothing to do with him. I barely know the guy.'

'Look, Lonnie. This isn't being recorded. I know you sent Weiss here.'

'You're nuts!'

'Something has changed the picture. We still have what Weiss came after. Who do we give them to?'

'Why don't you give them to Weiss? Whatever they are. From what I know about him, he keeps an agreement once he's made it.'

'Weiss is dead.'

Teed heard Raval's grunt of surprise. Raval said angrily, 'Friend, that's one hell of a way to conduct a negotiation.'

'But listen, Dennison didn't . . . '

'Shut up, Morrow. You make a choice and then you don't like it. The hell with that noise. That's no way to act.' There was righteous indignation in Raval's voice.

'Give me a chance to . . . '

'Tell that Dennison bastard he had his choice. Tell that Dennison bastard that it isn't any negotiation any more. Now it's personal. And tell him he can take those letters and he can . . . '

'Will you listen to me!'

'Go write up a petition, you son of a bitch.' The line clicked.

'Raval! Carboy did it. Raval! Hello!'

He hung the phone up slowly. 'Hung up on me. Wouldn't listen. Apparently he thinks we killed Weiss. You or I. He's sore. They're going to take it out on Jake.'

'No!' Marcia whispered, the back of her hand at her lips, eyes wide.

'Call back,' Powell said heavily. The

208

number was scribbled on the phone pad. Teed dialed again. The busy signal was a fast, acid bleat. He waited a few minutes and dialled again. After the phone rang six times, the Trowbridge girl answered.

'Let me talk to Raval again, please.'

'I'm sorry. Mr Raval has left.' She hung up.

'I'll move that car,' Teed said. 'Turn the house lights off, Marcia. We've got to have time. If the police come and take us down for questioning, we won't . . . '

'Where will you leave his car?' Marcia asked.

'I don't know. I'll find a place.'

'I'll follow you in your car and bring you back.'

'Good girl. Powell, while we're gone, see if you can get hold of Captain Herb Leighton. Get him over here, alone.'

He gave Marcia his keys. He started the big sedan and swung around her. In the rear-vision mirror he saw the lights of his car following. There was a sickish sweet smell inside the sedan. He rolled the window down, moved to the left so that the cold wind struck his face. Moving Weiss' body had reawakened the soreness in his abdomen, the pain of damaged muscles.

He avoided main streets, zigzagged through

209

the dark old residential section. He found a gas station with cars parked behind it, a night light over the pumps. He turned in behind the station, eased the sedan into a space between two cars. With his handkerchief he wiped the steering wheel, starter button, window crank. He got out and wiped the door handles he had touched. Marcia had parked across from the gas station, lights out, motor running.

When he opened the door, she slid over away from the wheel. As he started up, he thumbed open the glove compartment, took out two fresh packs of cigarettes, dropped them in her lap.

'If the law is there when we get back, we went out to buy those.'

'How can we find her, Teed? How can we know where to look?'

'Maybe Leighton will know. That's what I'm hoping.'

'And if he doesn't know? If we can't find her?'

'Don't think about it, Marse. We'll find her.'

He turned the last corner. A car was parked in front of the house. Teed pulled in behind it and they got out. As they went up on the porch, he looked through the glass door and saw the men who talked to Powell. Boyd, with the tape white across his nose. Pilcher with the battered hat shoved back, the match bobbing as he talked.

Teed caught Marcia and pulled her back. 'I'm getting out of here. When and if Leighton comes, whisper to him. Tell him that Rogale will know how to get in touch with me. I'll phone Rogale when I get to some place where I can phone.'

He walked quickly away from her, cutting across the yard, instinctively avoiding the place where Weiss had fallen.

The door of the police car opened. 'Hold it, you!' a voice said.

Teed recognized the tall young patrolman he had seen on the morning, a million years ago, when he had gone across to headquarters to check Miss Anderson's rumour about Felice Carboy. He couldn't remember the patrolman's name.

'Come over here. Where are you going?'

'What's the trouble, Officer?'

'We're investigating,' the man said importantly. 'Somebody heard shots around here. Say, you're Morrow, aren't you? Don't you get tired of having your neck out, mister? Go on in the house.'

'I want to show you something, Officer. Over here in the yard, below the broken railing. It might be blood.'

'Blood, eh?' the policeman said. 'Well, let's have a look.'

He made Teed walk ahead of him. Teed pointed to the spot. The man stared into the darkness, then bent down, reaching his fingers toward the indicated area. Teed pointed with his left hand. He took the automatic out of his pocket with his right hand and swung the flat of it against the side of the patrolman's head, over the left ear. It made a crisp sound. The man dropped to his hands and knees, moaned softly, and toppled over onto his side. Teed sprinted for his car, shoving the gun into his pocket. He had the car in motion almost before he slammed the door. He went down the street and gunned it around the corner, wheels spinning on the dry pavement.

The fear of the consequences of the act was a small thing compared to his fear for Jake Dennison.

12

There was silence on the line. When Armando Rogale spoke again, all the dullness of sleep had left his voice. 'Once again, Teed, and slower.'

'They grabbed Dennison's younger daughter. With her as a lever, Weiss came and broke Dennison down. He wrote two letters, copied two letters, that put him firmly in the bag. It was a trade. As Weiss left the house, Carboy killed him, walked down to his car and drove off. Apparently he followed Weiss.'

'Carboy!'

'Yes, Carboy. And Raval thinks Dennison killed Weiss, and we can't get hold of him to correct his impression. That leaves the daughter in a bad spot. Dennison was supposed to get hold of Leighton. While I was ditching Weiss' body, Pilcher and Boyd arrived to investigate. Somebody heard Carboy shoot Weiss. They didn't see me, but the driver did. I knocked the driver out and left. The older daughter is supposed to let Leighton know, if Powell was able to get hold of him, that he is to call you to find out where I am. I thought Leighton might have some idea of where the younger daughter is being held.'

'And where are you?'

'I'm in a booth in the bus station near the Fremont Theatre.'

'Good God! I hope to hell I'm dreaming all this.'

'You're not. Believe me.'

'Why did you hide Weiss' body? That was stupid!'

'Because,' Teed said patiently, 'we would have all been hauled off for questioning. And what would happen to Jake in the meantime?'

'Who is Jake?'

'The daughter, dammit! The one I'm going to find.'

'You're not safe in a bus station, Morrow. You've got to go to a better place than that. All I seem to be doing lately is hiding people. I'm running out of places. You know where Peterson Street is?'

'One of those streets that turn off Colony Avenue, isn't it?'

'Yes. There's a fire house on the corner. Two blocks down, second house on your left. The street door isn't locked. Push the bell for Fermi and walk up to the third floor. I'll tell them you're coming.'

'Who is it?'

'A cousin. What do you care? Don't leave

your car in front of the place, either.'

'I'm not that stupid, Armando.'

'I've got to be convinced. Get going. I'll see if I can contact Leighton.'

Teed went down Colony and parked three blocks beyond the fire house. He walked back and turned down Peterson. It was a depressing neighborhood. The tall narrow houses fronting on the sidewalk leaned against each other. Cats sang shrilly of love and passion. A man lurched down the sidewalk on the other side of the street, singing in a bass monotone.

The hall light was out and he had to use his lighter flame to find the button for Fermi. He pressed it, then went up the narrow wooden stairs, feeling his way. The hall light on the second floor was on. Someone was snoring thunderously, regularly. Across the hall a baby cried without heat, with merely a plaintive exhaustion.

As he reached the third floor a woman opened a door. It was a kitchen that opened onto the hall. She wore a bright red robe and her general shape was that of O.So glow's 'Little King.' Her face was swarthy, pyramidal, the eyes button bright.

'Mr Morrow,' she whispered, 'I am Anna Fermi. Come in, come in. And you sit there. Armando has called. He said you would need coffee. It has just been put on.'

She closed the door behind her, walked heavily to the gas range. He sat at the kitchen table. A fat puppy slept in a cardboard carton near the stove, his legs making twitching motions as he chased faraway rabbits in the tangled dreams of puppyhood.

'I don't like to impose on . . . '

She spun, her hands on the vast slabs of her hips, eyes crinkling. 'Impose! Impose! There is no such word. You are Armando's friend. This is his house.'

'His house?'

'He would deny it. Since my husband died, my husband who was his cousin, Armando has sent the money. Three boys I have. All little. Oldest ten. I work, but I cannot make much. So no talk of this imposing.'

'O.K.,' he said, returning her smile, liking her. The fat was deceptive. He saw that she was younger than he had first imagined. In her early thirties, possibly.

She frowned. 'Will you sleep here? That is a small problem.'

'I don't believe so, Mrs Fermi.'

'It can be done. I put two boys on the couch, and you can take their bed. In the extra bed is the girl.'

'The girl? Would her name be Barbara?'

'So! You know her! A good girl, and in bad

216

trouble, Armando says. She does not leave this place since . . . I must count . . . late on Wednesday. She says very little and she is sad and in the night I could hear her weeping because her bed is close to mine. She gave the money for the puppy. Fat Stuff, his name is. Now Barbara learns to make a spaghetti sauce.'

'I don't think you have to worry about my sleeping here. I'll just be here probably until Armando phones again.'

'Here is the coffee. Strong. Sugar?'

'No. Just as it is. And thanks. If you show me where the phone is, you can go back to bed, Mrs Fermi.'

'No, if you do not mind I will sit and have coffee. There may be something Armando will want. Tomorrow night, there will be no problem of the beds. Tomorrow Barbara goes, she said. Two boys go in my bed then, and you take the bed she is now using. I sleep in the room with the oldest boy. Are you hungry?'

'No, thank you.'

'Armando should marry. I tell him often. Too bad, I thought for one day that this Barbara, it was more than helping her only. So pretty a girl, and educated.'

'I don't think she'll be thinking of marriage for a while.'

The black eyes were shrewd. 'To forget one life, you should begin the new one very soon. She told me of herself. It was not something she had to tell, except that she thought she had to tell it.'

'She's a pretty confused girl, I guess.'

'We do not live in a very simple world any more. There are all kinds of shame in this world now. I wonder what kind is the worst. I do not think it is hers.'

'You are a good woman, Mrs Fermi.'

She chortled. 'Me? I'm just a practical woman who . . . Ssst!' She put a heavy hand on his wrist, heaved up out of her chair, caught the light cord and pulled it. Teed listened and heard the steps coming up the stairs.

She whispered, 'Anyone you do not want to see, I throw him down the stairs. In the neighborhood I am known as the violent woman. It is a handy thing sometimes.'

There was a light tap on the door. 'Anna? Open up for Armando.'

She pulled the light back on, opened the door. Armando hugged her, kissed her soundly. 'My God, Anna, you're an armful. Hi, Teed. How about a cup for me?'

'I am a woman of stature, merely,' Anna said with mock dignity. She plodded over to the cupboard, brought out another cup.

Armando sat down at the kitchen table. Teed noticed that there, in this room, his face was full of expression, that it had lost its impassivity. It was as though when he entered this apartment, he left behind the mask he wore for the world.

'Leighton is not to be found,' Armando said. 'Dennison couldn't get in touch with him. They've taken Dennison and the older daughter downtown. They've hauled cops out of bed and put them on duty. You and Carboy are the objects of what they usually call a 'city-wide search'.'

The door on the other side of the kitchen opened and Barbara Heddon came into the kitchen, her eyes slitted against the light. She said, 'I thought I recognised . . . ' And suddenly she recognised Teed. Her face went utterly blank.

'Hello, Barbara,' he said.

'Hello, Teed.' She wore dark blue pyjamas, a pale blue coolie coat buttoned high around her throat, falling in a straight line from her strong breasts to mid-thigh. She wore no make-up, and her face was kitten-soft with sleep. She said, 'Sorry,' and turned as though to leave.

'Come and sit down, Barbara,' Armando said. 'I think this is something you should know about.'

Anna started to get up. Barbara put a hand on her shoulder and pushed her gently back into the chair, got her own cup and filled it at the pot on the stove. She sat at Teed's right, and did not look at him. Her hands were steady as she poured the cream. Teed looked at them and thought how fine and strong they were.

'Suppose you tell her, Teed,' Armando said.

'Maybe she'd rather not hear it.'

'If Armando thinks I should,' she said softly, 'I think you better tell me.'

Anna said, 'I would go and leave you three with privacy, but it is too much work to stand up, and the coffee is good, even if I made it myself.'

'Stay, Anna,' Armando said, patting her thick hand.

Teed told the story as quickly and factually as he could. He did not leave out Jake's infatuation for him and her fear for him, the factors which had trapped her. He looked down at his right hand as he spoke, and saw that the hurried scrubbing in the bus terminal had not removed the darkness from around the nails of his first and second fingers.

He took the picture out of his pocket and handed it to Armando, on his left. Armando looked at it, lips compressed. 'And here are the letters,' Teed said. 'I'm glad I didn't leave them with Powell.'

Armando read them slowly, carefully. As he read, Anna said, 'It is a foul thing. It is a low and evil thing. To use a young girl. To give her shame. To break the heart of her father.'

Barbara said, with harshness in her tone, 'I think I know why you wanted me to hear this, Armando.'

'It isn't something I can ask you to do, Barbara,' Armando said, keeping his eyes steady on hers.

'What is this all about?' Teed asked.

Barbara looked squarely at him for the first time since she had entered the room. 'Armando knows that I'm trying to make a clean break with my bawdy past, Teed. He's too much of a gentleman to ask me this sort of a favour. He thinks that I know enough about the operations of the vice ring here in Deron so that I can make a guess as to where she is and help you get to her.'

Anna put her hand over Barbara's. 'In your words and the way you look, you are beating yourself with whips. Don't.'

'We're thinking about that girl, Anna. Not me. Here's the picture, Armando. Maria Gonzalez is the . . . co-ordinator, I suppose you'd call it. She handles the call-girl list. She doesn't run a house, but she sets up the amount of cut that each house pays in.

Girls that are . . . recruited here never stay here in a house or, if they're the 'superior type' ' . . . Barbara's lip twisted in an ugly way . . . 'They don't go on the local call list. They keep the house girls moving, and the eastern syndicate does the 'booking', I suppose you'd call it. A call-girl has more freedom of action. Maria's people root out the amateurs, and either get co-operation, or make certain they get sent up for a while.

'The thing they keep the quietest about is the recruiting. Any one of the men who work with Weiss and Stratter can get a bonus by putting the finger on local talent that might make a professional. The police recruit too. You know. 'I'll send you to a friend and we'll forget this charge against you'. Some of the girls are eager to join the team. Some are a little reluctant. I know that they all get an interview with Maria before they go on the booking list to some town down the valley, or out of the state. Because there's always the chance of trouble, the recruits are taken out of town. That would be the safest place for them to take the Dennison girl. It's a place on Route 63, this side of Broganville, called the Castle Ann. The wise boys and girls call it 'the training camp'.'

'I know the place,' Armando said. 'An old country hotel on a hill, with a bar off the lobby. It's got a stone wall around it . . . '

'And barbed wire,' she said, 'and guards on the gate. Maria has a broken-down photographer out there with a darkroom and all. I understand they make movies there, too. For the smoker trade. It would fit.'

'Just a minute,' Teed said. 'We've even got proof. That's what Weiss started to say before he stopped himself. Castle Ann. Let's go get her.'

'Sit down, Teed,' Armando snapped. 'Nobody is just going to run out there and grab her. Obviously Raval has brought in some out-of-town talent. With things popping this way, he'd be silly not to. And where do you think those boys hang out? Castle Ann just happens to be Raval's little fortress. They got everything but a moat and a drawbridge. You go riding out there in your little tin suit of armour and they'll make you eat your white horse.'

'But while we're sitting here . . . '

'Let me think a minute.'

'How about the FBI?' Teed demanded. 'Kidnapping is federal, isn't it?'

'With the girl insisting that she's staying there of her own free will?'

'And the local cops are no good,' Teed said.

'Oh, they're fine. All they're doing is hunting for you,' Barbara said, 'I was out

223

there . . . for a little while, after Maria came to the jail to see me. I know this. It would take a small army to get in there by force. But if a person was known . . . '

Armando patted her hand. 'I was afraid I was going to have to ask you, Barbara.'

'What can she do?' Teed demanded angrily.

'The thing to do is to get word to the girl, of course. She can tell the Dennison girl that what they're using on her to hold her there is just a bluff. Then I could make a legitimate kidnapping charge. Barbara, do you think you could get to see her?'

'That's going to depend on who is out there, Mr Rogale. If Maria Gonzales is out there, it isn't going to work very well.'

'That's a hell of a risk for you to take,' Teed said. 'I don't like it.'

She smiled wanly at him. 'I'm a lot better able to take care of myself than that Dennison kid is.'

'You aren't going to be popular out there, Barbara.'

'It's worth the risk. Maybe, if I'm lucky, I can get her out of there. Say that Maria sent me to bring her to town.'

'I'll drive you out,' Armando said. 'If you can't work it, I'll come in after you and try a bluff of my own.'

'I'm coming along,' Teed said firmly.

'You are staying right here,' Armando said, with equal firmness.

'I can be useful, dammit.'

'In what way? Kicking a hole in the stone wall? Or catching bullets in your teeth? What's your speciality?'

'You can't stop me from coming along,' Teed said.

Armando gave him a long stare and then shrugged. 'O.K., O.K. We can't spare the time to argue with you. Go get dressed, Barbara.'

She dressed quickly, returned to the kitchen wearing a grey wool suit, a short fox jacket. She opened her purse and held it so that Armando could look into it. 'I'm taking this along,' she said.

'A toy thing like that?'

'It's twenty-five calibre and I know how to use it.'

'You don't want the kind of trouble that can bring you.'

She put her purse down, held up a small mirror, carefully painted her lips, compressed them, examined the result. 'I'm taking it along,' she said. 'In my whole life I've been frightened of only one person. Maria Gonzales. I'm taking it along.'

Anna came to her, put her hands on Barbara's shoulders, looked intently into her face. 'You come back here. Stay for as long as you want.'

Barbara's face softened. 'Thank you, Anna.'

'And you are not making the sauce right yet. Practice you need.'

'Thank you for everything.'

Anna hugged her. 'Such a silly girl,' she said.

The puppy awoke and whined. His tail whapped against the side of the carton. They went down the stairs and out onto the dark sidewalk. Armando walked around his car, slid in behind the wheel. Barbara sat in the middle.

Before he started the car, Armando said, 'If you want to go back upstairs, Barbara, we'll both understand. And we'll think of another scheme.'

'I want to do it,' she said. Her voice was remote. 'I have to do it, I guess. You can't just stop thinking and stop remembering. The scales are all out of balance for me. I have to put a little weight on the other side of them.'

Armando said, 'Good girl.' He started the motor and they moved slowly down the street.

'I liked your note, Barbara,' Teed said.

She gave him a smile, quick and pallid in the darkness of the car, barely visible in the glow of the dash lights.

Armando drove with extreme care. Route

63 left Deron at the southwest edge of the city. It was two-lane asphalt, crossed by many spur tracks that led to sleeping factories. Beyond the tracks was a mile of grubby drive-ins, gas stations, beer joints. And then the road began to lift into the hills, began to curve through farmland. The faint spice of Barbara's perfume was in his nostrils and her knee touched his. He increased the pressure a tiny bit and she took her knee away. It made him remember the perfume Jake had swiped from Marcia, made him remember the absurd reek of her in the darkness, the pathetic youngness.

Armando pulled over to the shoulder. 'We'll get out here, Barbara. Once we're over the next hill, the gate guard might notice the car stop and start wondering.'

Armando got out and Barbara slid under the wheel. Teed put his hand on her arm. 'Be careful. Please be careful.'

She turned to Armando, who stood at the window, beside her. 'Don't you two try anything foolish. I'll try to be out in twenty minutes. If I'm not out of there by then, you'll know I'm . . . not coming out for a while. Then you head back for the city and get help. I *will* be held against my will.'

'You were thinking of that angle from the beginning?' Armando asked.

She said, 'Yes.' Her voice was low. 'Please get out, Teed.'

He stepped down into the shallow ditch. The car moved back out onto the asphalt, up the slope, over the crest.

'Very special gal,' Armando said. 'A very gutsy young lady. That'll teach me to go around judging people too fast.'

'If Maria Gonzales is there, it will be bad?'

'Maria has a temper. And a knife.'

'We shouldn't have let her try it, Armando.'

'She's special, Teed. But she's still expendable.'

'I wonder.'

'Let's get as close to the gate as we can.'

13

After the motor sound faded, the countryside silence was like a blanket across the stars. Wind skittered through the dry grass. Dried leaves rustled. A distant rooster crowed in sleepy protest.

'How do we stand on time?' Teed asked.

'She's been gone three minutes. At twenty of four her time will be up.'

'And then what?'

'Then we can try a bluff.'

'A good idea?'

'Frankly, Morrow, it stinks. But the alternative is heading back for town on foot and trying to talk somebody into sticking Uncle Sam's neck out for the sake of one of our local call-girls. That stinks too.'

They crossed the ditch and walked beside the fence. 'Lights coming from town,' Armando said tersely. 'Flatten out.'

They stretched out beside a rusty wire fence. The car boomed by. It dropped over the crest and reappeared later, twin red taillights sliding up a far slope. Teed got up. Something pricked his knee. He picked a cluster of burrs out of his trouser leg.

'This the Castle Ann fence?' Teed asked.

'No. They really *have* a fence. See where it starts up at the crest there?'

At the top of the crest there was a place where they could see over the high wall. It was a four-storey oblong — a frame building that sat on the top of a small knoll about two hundred feet from the road. Some windows were lighted on the two top floors. Lights were visible in all the windows of the far end of the main floor.

'See those ground-floor lights? The bar is in that end.'

There were no trees around the structure. It had a curiously naked look. 'Why four stories out in the middle of nowhere?' Teed asked.

'A farmer built it in the early twenties. The kindest thing you could say about him was that he was slightly eccentric. He made dough in the first war. Always wanted to live in a hotel. So he had one built. A few salesmen stopped there until the old guy decided he didn't like guests in his hotel. He lived there alone, getting screwier every year. When he decided people were laughing at him he had the big stone fence built, with barbed wire on the top. Had all the trees cut down. He'd sit up in a fourth-floor room and fire a shotgun in the air whenever anybody stopped by the gate. When he died, in the thirties, a couple bought it cheap, and went broke trying to run it as a restaurant. Later, one of Raval's front men bought it. It's ideal for them. No interruptions. It's outside the city, and the county cops don't bother with it. It has been raided a couple of times by narcotics people. But they didn't find a thing. Take a good look and memorise as much of it as you can, Teed. This is the last look we'll get at it until we get inside the wall. Better whisper from here on.'

They moved cautiously down toward the gate, staying close to the wall.

Armando stopped, his back against the wall. He put his lips close to Teed's ear. 'We're thirty feet from the gate. Time is three-thirty-two. Can you spot the guard?'

As Teed watched there was a puzzling glow that lasted a few seconds, and then a click, clearly audible.

'Cigarette lighter,' Armando whispered.

The smell of tobacco drifted down the night wind, verifying the guess. Teed wanted a cigarette badly. He took the automatic out of his coat pocket, shoved it inside his belt.

'Four more minutes,' Armando whispered.

Teed's nerves were drawn tight. There was a hollow feeling in his middle. It had been easy enough to think of taking on Castle Ann singlehanded when he had been back in the city. But now it was a place where you could go behind a high wall and be suddenly taken dead. Both the girls were in there. And from the hilltop he had seen the shiny cars flanked near the bar.

Armando put his mouth close to Teed's ear again. 'Rumour has it that several people who became objectionable to Raval are planted behind that wall. Look, stay right where you are.'

'But . . . '

'Shut up. You'll be able to hear how it goes.'

Armando walked silently up the hill, away from the gate. Teed waited, puzzled. Armando crossed the ditch, reversed his direction, and came noisily down the road, heels clacking loudly.

He walked right up to the gate. Teed saw the flashlight catch Armando full in the face.

'Get the light out of my eyes,' Armando demanded in an irritated tone.

'Where do you think you're going, friend?' a deep voice asked.

'I'm trying to get a phone. My car ran out of gas about a mile back.'

'I seen you some place.'

'Get the light out of my eyes!'

The light shifted down to the ground at Armando's feet. 'What do you want a phone for?'

'I want to call up the Vassar field hockey squad. We're all going to dance barefoot on your dewy grass.'

'Wise, eh? This is private property. Where did I see you before?'

'Maybe you want my birth certificate. What kind of a place is this? Just let me go phone, will you?'

'Say, aren't you Rogale?' the guard asked.

'So skip it,' Armando said. 'I'll try the next place.' He started to move back. The light caught him in the face again.

'You just stand nice and still, Mr Rogale. People are going to be glad to see you. They're going to want to know why you're nosing around. Now stand still while I get the gate open.'

Teed moved slowly, quietly down toward the gate. The gun was going to be no good. A shot would ruin what feeble chances they had. Teed heard a metallic clack, a creak of hinges. The man moved out into view, gun and flashlight pointed at Armando.

Teed fumbled in the grass, found a pebble. He flipped it over the guard's head so that it landed in the grass beyond the gate. As the guard's head turned, Teed tried to reach him in four running strides. But the moment that he had turned, Armando had kicked the man lustily in the pit of the stomach. As the guard bent forward from the waist, Armando laced his fingers around the back of the man's neck, yanked down hard as he raised his knee. The guard fell with a thud that drove the air out of him.

'Quick and efficient,' Teed said.

'I grew up in a rough neighborhood. Haven't hit anybody in six years. Thought I'd forgotten how.'

Armando found the flashlight, swept the beam around until he located the gun. He searched the man. 'Gun and a sap. Which do you want?'

'Take them both. I've got Weiss' automatic.'

'Are we thinking along the same lines?' Armando said in a low tone.

There was unsteadiness in Teed's voice as he answered, 'There isn't much else to do, is there? I'm scared.'

'And you are not alone. Help me drag him inside. We'll leave him in the brush. First let me give him this.' The sap made a small dull sound as Armando swung it.

They dragged him through the gate, off to one side. Armando opened the gate wide, said, 'We'll leave the gate like this. I don't know how much time we'll have. I think another guard patrols the fence line. Any ideas?'

'Just move fast, see if we can find both girls, and try to get out. Go ahead. You know the layout.'

The drive was of coarse gravel. They walked on the grass beside the drive. A hundred feet from the gate Armando veered sharply to the left. They circled the lighted windows. They could not see in.

'Eight cars, not counting mine,' Armando said in a low tone. 'How do you like those odds? If the Bar Association could only see me now. Let's hope for an unlocked back door. I'm trying to pretend I'm Humphrey Bogart. Who are you?'

Teed laughed softly, nervously. 'Henry Aldrich.'

'You a good shot?'

'At a target. I've never tried people.'

At the rear of the building Armando risked using the flashlight. He narrowed the beam by shielding part of it off with his hand. He swept the narrow beam across a battered row of garbage cans. They were overflowing and the stench was rancid, nauseous. There was a secondary odour of faulty plumbing. The light touched the bottom step of a short flight that led up to a back stoop, a narrow door. Armando tiptoed up the steps and tried the door. He came back down.

'Not that way,' he said softly.

It was the only door in the rear of the building. As they reached the back corner on the end opposite the bar music blasted out into the night, freezing them in their tracks for a moment. An old Armstrong that Teed knew well. Gravel-voice, sweet and true.

'That means people in the bar,' Armando said tautly.

'A window?' Teed asked, above the music sound.

'Too high, and too risky!'

Armando stepped around the corner of the building and then tried to dodge back, treading so heavily on Teed's instep that he made an involuntary gasp of pain. Armando stared, then let out a long sigh. 'It's O.K.'

A man stood, face to the building, spread-legged, one arm flat against the wall, forehead against his forearm. He made a dry retching sound.

As they watched he fell to his knees, struggled up again. He moaned.

He paid no attention to them as they walked around him. Armando paused after they were by him. 'I wonder,' he said.

'What's the matter?'

'Sometimes those people get in the way. They get well too quick!' He shrugged, took

236

two quick steps and swung the sap. The man slid down the wall, face first, and rolled over onto his side.

'Who is he?'

'Belongs to Stratter. Drives for him sometimes. Come on!'

The front door was on ground level. Armando raised his head cautiously and looked through the glass. He beckoned to Teed. Teed stood beside him and looked in. Three wide wooden steps six feet inside the door led up to the lobby. Directly opposite the lobby a stairway went to the floors above. The lobby was dark, but the bar lights shone through an open door.

The music was louder.

The bar lights made a bright wide streak through the lobby, ending at the deserted desk.

'Maybe nobody is looking into the lobby,' Armando said. 'But we got to figure they are. If we sneak, somebody will investigate. Can you walk across like you owned the place?'

'I can try!'

A man's heavy laugh came from the bar. The music ended. Armando, his hand on the door, paused. There was silence in which Teed could hear conversation, a woman's voice taking part, rising high and shrill. And the music started again. The same piece.

Somebody liked it.

'Like you owned the place,' Armando said, pushing the door open.

The board floor was bare. They walked across the light path. Out of the corner of his eye Teed saw a smoky room, the corner of a dark-stained bar, a big round table with a group sitting at it, a shirt-sleeved man with a cigar carrying a tin tray of drinks to the table.

They passed the light. They were almost to the stairs when somebody in the bar yelled, 'Hey! Who's that out there?'

Armando yelled back, in whining falsetto, 'It's Greta Garbo, you stupid jerk.'

'Wise guy,' the man bellowed. The others laughed at him. The man didn't come out to investigate.

Halfway up the stairs to the wide landing, Armando whispered, 'Stratter is in there. And that is not good.'

'Where do we go from here?'

'Eyes and ears open. I can't think of anything else.'

The second-floor hallway stretched the long way of the building, with a window at each end, doors opening off both sides of the hall. Teed counted nine doors on a side. Eighteen rooms. Three floors. Fifty-four rooms to wonder about, to search.

The hall was carpeted. Armando started in

one direction. He held his ear close to the first door, motioned Teed to head the other way and do the same. The first two rooms were silent. In the third he heard a woman saying, ' . . . so I told Joe that if that was the way he was going to act about it, he could damn well kiss . . . '

He tiptoed around the door. At the last door he listened and heard a girl's muted, helpless crying, pillow-muffled. His heart gave a great leap. He tried the knob. The door was locked. He looked back and motioned to Armando. Armando came quickly and silently down the hall. He listened for a moment. He tapped cautiously on the door.

There was a creak of bed springs and a ribbon of light appeared under the door. Steps came close to the door.

'Whaddya want?' a tear-dulled voice asked beyond the thin panel.

Armando looked at Teed and raised one eyebrow. Teed shook his head regretfully.

'Let me in a minute, baby,' Armando said.

'You go tell her I'm not going to do it. You go tell her I'm not going to let nobody else in here no matter what she says she'll do to me.'

'Not so loud, baby,' Armando said. 'This isn't what you think. There's two of us here. We want to help you. No kidding.'

'Oh, sure,' she said bitterly.

'I want to find out about another girl who might be here,' Teed said. The door panel was so thin that they could hear the thick catch in her breathing, the aftermath of sobs.

A key turned in the lock and the door swung open a crack. She looked at them, prepared to slam it again. She seemed reassured.

'O.K., so come in,' she said.

The room was drab and unpleasant. A metal bed frame painted white. A round hooked rug so ancient and soiled that it was all of a colour — a fetid brown. A stand with a cracked marble top. A white pitcher, tin wash basin, scabbed soap dish. A pile of clean threadbare towels on the lower shelf of the wash stand. There was no other furniture in the room except for the flimsy unpainted chest of drawers, a round bleary mirror fastened over it.

The girl had a ripe sturdy body, a long pale Mediterranean face, enormous dark eyes. She wore a too-tight cerise house coat that zipped from throat to ankles. Her dark hair was an unpleasant tangle and there was a bruise under her right eye.

Armando spoke to her in rapid Italian. She answered in kind, and then, as she continued to answer, the phrases grew more broken, disjointed. Tears spilled out of the huge dark

240

eyes. She sat on the edge of the bed, put her face in her hands, continued to talk, her voice muffled, torn.

Armando asked soft questions. She answered them, some with anger, some apathetically.

Armando turned to Teed. His eyes were angry. 'I know of her people. Labouring people. It's a tired old story. A very ordinary story. The boy she was going to marry married somebody else. She dated a man who came often to the restaurant where she worked. She didn't care what happened to her any more. He took her on a business trip to Buffalo with him. Then he brought her out here and turned her over to Maria. She's ashamed to go home and she's lost her job. She expects to be taken away with another girl in the morning. A man is going to drive them to another city. Scranton, she thinks. I know the man who left her here. She was drunk when he left her here. His name is Kissler and he's been indicted for small things, and never convicted. She's been here three nights. The only girl she knows is the Polish girl who is being taken away with her in the morning. And, of course, Maria.'

The girl lifted a tortured face. She touched her fingertips to the bruise on her cheek. There was hate in her face, mingled with fear.

'Won't her family notify the police?'

'She wrote them a letter. Maria dictated it. They won't make a fuss.'

'We better try the next floor.'

Armando spoke to her again, this time in English. 'Keep your door locked. I think if we're lucky we can get you out of here. And no one will have to know where you've been.'

'Skip it,' she said. 'I'm all right here. Maybe I like it.'

Teed pulled the door shut. She sat on the bed staring after them as if she hated them. He wondered if she did.

They made the next floor without incident. The juke music was fainter. The tune had been changed. Boogiewoogie dirge. Lament for a fallen lady. A room door was open. Two girls in housecoats sat on the bed. Their eyes were vacant with liquor, heavy glass tumblers in their hands.

'Go 'way, palsies. We're busy. We're on vacation,' a puffy blonde said.

'We're looking for a tall dark girl who came in tonight, early.'

'Go ask Duchess Maria, palsy. You got a special choice, go ask the old bag.'

They both giggled. Their mouths looked smashed. Their eyes were as empty as tunnels on an abandoned railroad.

'Where's the Duchess?' Armando asked.

The blonde pointed at the ceiling. 'You new or something? Upstairs, brother. Your friend's kinda cute. You go look for the Duchess and leave him here. We'll buy him a drink.'

They listened at the other rooms on the third floor. They were all dark, silent.

Teed whispered, 'She could be in any one of these. Drugged or something.'

'I know it. Come on. We need a break.'

Halfway up the stairs they beard a sound like the snap of a distant twig. Armando paused. 'That come from up above?'

'It sounded that way. Come on.'

They went up to the top floor. The floor plan was different than on the two floors below. Evidently there had been a halfhearted attempt to make a ballroom out of the open space at the head of the stairs. Overhead was a cartwheel chandelier with three lighted bulbs in it. The corners of the room were in shadow. Two walls, the front and back of the building, were windows. There were two doors in each of the end walls. Light shone under both doors at one end.

Though they tried to walk quietly, their footsteps resounded in the big room. Overhead hand-hewn beams slanted up to the roof peak.

When they were twenty feet from the

243

doors, the one on the left opened and a tall woman stepped out. She stopped abruptly. The chandelier light was full on her face. Her mature body was tightly sheathed in a silver gown that left her shoulders bare. Her hair, shining black, was pulled tightly back, so tightly that it gave her eyes an almost oriental tilt. The bone structure of her face made Teed think of a Dolores del Rio, but the mouth was not right. It was large and ripe and brutal and harsh. She held a handkerchief in her left hand, held her left fist tightly against her side, under her heart. Her right hand was lost in the folds of the silver skirt.

'What . . . what do you want?'

'You are Maria Gonzales, I believe,' Armando said.

'The light is behind you, I do not . . . '

'I think you know me. I'm Armando Rogale. And this is Teed Morrow. Where is the Dennison girl?'

After a few moments she laughed. Her voice was a girl's voice when she laughed.

'You are too late. She has been taken back to her father. She was a silly child to come out here.'

'You won't mind if we look around, then?'

'You don't belong here. Go back downstairs.'

Teed watched her closely as they moved

nearer. She pulled the corners of her brutal mouth down in an odd grimace and shut her eyes for a moment, then opened them wide. Her voice grew stronger.

'Get out of here! Both of you!'

Armando was the closest. She backed up, swayed a bit, her back striking the door jamb.

'Get out of the way, Maria,' Armando said softly.

Teed looked at her left hand. Since they had begun to talk, a dark stain had begun to spread below her hand.

'Look, she's hurt,' Teed said.

Armando reached out and grasped her left wrist. As he pulled it free of her body, she spun toward him and struck with the incredible explosive fury of a great cat. She struck with the right hand that she had been holding at her side. Teed saw the glint of metal and he was too late to cry out a warning. Armando took three slow steps backward, his face vacant with surprise. He reached his right hand up and tentatively fingered the dark hilt of the switch knife that protruded from his chest on the left side. The handle pointed down toward the floor. Maria stood silent, her eyes smoking.

Armando reached around the hilt and touched his shoulder, slid his hand back. He said calmly, 'The bitch missed. I think it went up under the collar bone. The point is sticking right out through my coat.'

'Don't try to pull it out. Leave it there.'

They looked at Maria. She still held her side, and her eyes were shut. Her face twisted for a moment and then cleared. She pushed herself away from the doorframe and walked between them, taking careful steps. Her heavy hips swayed under the silver gown. She left the door open behind her. She wavered once and regained her balance.

They could sense the extent of the effort she was making. It was hypnotic, to watch that hard, unemotional determination. She planted her foot on the first step, took another step. She stood motionless for a frozen breath of time, then slowly lowered her head until her chin was on her chest. She bent forward from the waist, as though seeking to examine something hidden on the stair below her. And she followed the direction of the slow bow, pitching down, falling with slack weight on the splinter-rough edges of the uncarpeted stairs, falling with a sound of wooden hammers. Her head and shoulders caught somehow, and they saw her legs go over, the silver skirt falling away, the dim light shining on the puffed white flesh of calf and thigh, and then she was below the floor level, out of sight. The sound went on, endlessly, flesh-thud and bone-hammer. There was a stillness, a pad of running feet in the third floor hallway, a phlegm-throated gargling scream.

'I'll get you out of here,' Teed said to Armando.

'Not yet. Can't move my left arm without crying, but I'm OK.'

They went quickly through the door Maria had left open. Armando turned and covered the stairs. 'Take a look around,' he said.

It was not an apartment. It was merely two very well-furnished rooms. Off-white rugs and eggplant draperies and driftwood finish on the furniture, with here and there a touch of Chinese red to kill the deadness of grey and off-white. A dozen floor lamps and table lamps with opaque shades threw light downward, so that the reflection from the off-white rugs had an indirect lighting effect.

It looked like what it undoubtedly was — the private pleasure palace of a stone-hard ruthless woman — the one place where she could unbend, where she could forget she had the soul of a comptometer and remember that she had the flesh and body of a woman.

'Hurry it up!' Armando called huskily, the ripe edge of his baritone softened by pain.

In each of the two rooms there was a huge pillowed couch-bed. Teed went into the second room and saw, beyond the edge of the couch-bed, the woman's hand, endlessly opening and shutting, palm down, fingernails making a soft scrabbling in the pile of the pale rug.

He ran to her and stopped when he saw the bloody mask of face. The hair, the long body belonged to Barbara. The face was ruin. She rolled hips and shoulders slowly from side to side and scrabbled at the rug with both hands in the aimless metronome of pain. There was a thin burned taste in the air and he identified it when he saw the small gun a yard away. The gun had been the snapping of the stick. The gun had been the long stairway tumble.

He knelt beside her. 'Barbara! Barbara, it's Teed.'

A long wedge of flesh folded down from the left cheek, exposing the white molars. He saw what had happened. The bleeding was not profuse. The girl had been slashed across the face twice, possibly three times.

The open cheek gave her voice a flat whistling quality. 'Missed her, Teed. Shot and missed her and she . . . had the knife . . . '

'You didn't miss her.'

'Teed, my face. I can't see, Teed.'

'That's all right,' he said gently. 'We'll get you to a hospital. It's just the blood that

. . . keeps you from seeing.'

'Teed, I hurt. I hurt so bad.'

'Don't worry about it, honey.'

'They're coming!' Armando called.

Barbara seemed to hear him. 'Teed, the girl! I found where she is, Teed The other side of the big room. Locked in over there, Teed. I . . . I almost got away with it. Maria was too smart. Be careful, Teed. There's someone with her, I think.'

'I'll get her and come back for you, darling.'

But once again she was beyond hearing or caring. She rolled slowly from side to side, moving her body but not her head.

There was a shot that made a vast hollow boom and the echoes rolled for seconds from raftered ceiling to high walls of the big room. A man yelled hoarsely and there was the sound of another fall on the stairs.

14

Armando lay on his belly on the floor inside the first room, the gun aimed around the edge of the doorframe toward the top of the stairs. He was propped up on his left arm so that the knife hilt wouldn't touch the floor. Pain had greyed his face. But he grinned and his teeth were startling white in the mask of pain.

'Now, as we jolly old British say, we're for it. Don't show a whisker in that doorway.'

'You're even beginning to look like Bogart.'

'I bet he never felt like this. Stage blood he uses.' Armando winced. 'And he always looks so happy. I think I just killed somebody. He ran up the stairs and he had a gun in his hand, so I fired. He just flopped right down out of sight. I'm darn close to being sick to my stomach.'

A slug slammed into the doorframe. The hammer-blow impact was a distinct sound above the noise of the shot.

'Barbara is in there. Cut to hell.'

Armando's eyes narrowed. 'Dead?'

'Disfigured. Slashed across the face a few times. She told me Jake is across the way.

I'm going over there.'

They listened, heard the murmur of voices on the stairs.

'O.K., Teed. Run like hell. I'll keep them down.'

He backed up from the doorway, then started running, bursting through the doorway into the ballroom at full speed, running well up on his toes. He counted two quick-spaced shots, then a third that smashed glass, made a tinkling somewhere on his left. Without slackening speed or changing stride, he doubled his fists across his chest, turned and hit the door with his right shoulder, hitting it as close to the frame on the knob side as he could. The door exploded inwards with a rip of torn wood. He tripped and rolled over and over in the darkness, his shoulder numbed. Something metallic and angular fell across him, struck his hand painfully. He thrust it aside and stood up. The room was dark. The light from the ballroom chandelier made a pale path across the bare floor.

'Jake!' he called sharply. In the dimness he could see camera tripods, dingy velvet backdrops. It was a tripod that had fallen across him when he rolled into it.

'Jake!' he called. There was no answer. He did not know where to find the lights.

He heard a deep male groan, a stirring in the darkness. He whirled, aiming the gun. He peered into the shadows, advanced cautiously, made out the figure of a man, face down near a shapeless cot. Teed crouched by him, flicked on the lighter, rolled the man over. He had a gross face, a beard stubble, a bloody welt over one ear. Beside his head lay a small heavy camera in a leather case. Someone had swung it by the strap.

Two shots awoke the heavy echoes again, resonating through the high-ceilinged ballroom. He straightened up and called her again. One of the windows at the far end of the room was open. The sleazy curtain flickered in the night wind. He ran to the window, leaned out and looked down. There was a paleness down there, a crumpled thing that lay across the hood of one of the ranked cars. A big car. The light from one of the bar windows on the ground floor touched the figure and he saw how dark was her hair, remembered how the hair had felt between his fingers. Time stopped for him as he stared down, knowing from the position of the figures, from the utter stillness, that no one need hurry for Jake again. Ever.

The man groaned again. Teed walked woodenly back to him. He slapped the man into consciousness, put the muzzle of the automatic full against his face. He willed himself to pull the trigger, to let the slug slam the man into a ragdoll limpness. The man inched backward along the floor and whispered, 'No, no, no.'

Teed tried to pull the trigger. He could not do it. He despised himself for being unable to do it. He swung the gun, using the arm motion of a softball pitcher. He held the gun flat on his palm and it smashed into the point of the chin of the whimpering man. He felt the bone go under the blow. He snatched the gun up and stood for a moment. He walked to the doorway, kicked the sagging door out of the way.

Armando yelled, 'Get down, Teed. Down!'

A head appeared above floor level, ducked down again. A splinter whined off the doorframe, inches from his shoulder. As he started to walk toward the stairs, the gun held rigidly in front of him, his steps slow and steady, Teed thought of a girl who rolled from side to side with pain, her fingers scrabbling at the white rug.

He thought of another girl who had fallen through the cool night.

From somewhere far away he heard Armando shout another warning, then curse and fire toward the stairs. Now he could see down into the dark stair well. He lifted the gun to eye level and aimed carefully at the heart of the moving shadows. He fired and a man screamed. He took another step and fired again. Something hot pinched at Teed's thigh, as though a gigantic crab claw had closed on it, the sharpness penetrating front and back. It threw him off stride. After the hard pinch came a warm wetness on his leg.

He fired with each step he took and then there was no movement on the stairs. Just some still shadows.

Someone pulled hard at his arm. He turned and pulled the trigger. The gun clicked. Armando knocked the gun aside.

'What's the matter with you?' he screamed. 'You look like a crazy man. What are you trying to do?'

'I'm going down.'

'With an empty gun?'

'I'm going down.'

Armando's hard palm bounced off his cheek. 'Wake up! What was wrong in there?'

'Jake's dead,' he said.

Armando whistled softly. He stared hard at Teed. 'For a minute we got control. You cleared the stairs. Look. Two of them there. Who do you think you are? Bogart?'

Teed shook his head hard, to swing the mists out of his mind. He tried to smile. 'All right, Armando. What do we do now?'

'I think we're supposed to try to retain the initiative. So we both go down. Follow pretty close.'

Teed followed him. His foot scuffed a gun, knocking it from one step to the next lower one. He picked it up quickly, dropping the other. Armando went down the stairs with extreme caution, flattened against the wall. He stopped one step up from the third-floor level. Teed was behind him. Ahead was the blank wall of the other side of the corridor. To their left was the railing, the next flight going down to the second floor. To reach it without exposing themselves to anyone standing in the hall, they would have to go over the railing. Teed sensed that the knife wound had weakened Armando to the point where this would be difficult if not impossible. And his own wounded leg was growing less reliable with frightening speed.

'Morrow!' someone called, surprisingly close.

'What do you want, Raval?' Armando asked in a pleasant, conversational tone.

They both heard the grunt of surprise, the soft scuffle as people moved back quickly.

'Rogale,' Raval said, with the same casual confidence that Teed remembered from the terrace on a sunny morning. 'What are we? Kids, yet? Buck Rogers, maybe? We have some hard boys here. You start shooting, they start shooting, and it makes trouble. We got Maria dead down here and one out-of-town boy, and two boys with holes in them.'

'And two dead men at the head of the stairs,' Teed said tonelessly, 'and a girl with a slashed face and a dead girl.'

'Dead girl?' Raval asked uneasily.

'Miss Dennison went out the window, Raval,' Teed said.

Raval cursed softly. Then he said, 'That tears it good, but we can still put a lid on it, boys. We can still stop going bang bang. I'll give both you boys a good piece of change and then we can burn this place down. It will burn good. Tragic deaths in fire. There'll still be a stink, but not so bad we can't sit it out.'

'Better listen to the boss,' a new voice said.

'That's Stratter,' Armando whispered to Teed.

A car motor roared into life. They heard the wheels skid on gravel, the sound of the car fading rapidly away.

'Well?' Raval called.

'I'm ashamed of you, Lonnie,' Armando said. 'A nice country-club member like you. A guy with his daughters in a fancy school. They say you've got thirty suits of clothes. Is that right? Nice going for a reform-school graduate.'

Raval's voice thickened. 'Take your choice, boys. You burn with it if you don't want to play.'

'How is that going to read?' Armando asked. 'Joint burns down. A joint owned, indirectly, by Lonnie Raval. Dead in the fire are prominent young attorney, the Assistant City Manager, the daughter of the City Manager, and a choice collection of assorted muscle men. You're licked no matter how you play it, Lonnie. It's gone too far already. The eastern syndicate is going to be very, very annoyed with you. Don't you follow orders? I thought the policy was to go as legitimate as possible while all this Senate committee stuff is still hot. And here you are, kidnapping people, shooting people, burning people up. Tsk, tsk.'

There was a mumbling whisper they couldn't catch, then Stratter said, 'You want it done, you do it yourself this time.'

Another car left, noisily.

Armando, said, 'Be smart, Stratter. The others are pulling out. Raval is through. And here's something. We can't get out, and neither can you. You can't get to the stairs going down any more than we can. Slap him down, Stratter, and I'll see that it counts in your favour.'

'Get back, Stratter,' Raval said in a

colourless voice. 'Get back.'

Someone ran noisily down one of the lower flights, raced across the lobby. A door slammed.

'There goes some more,' Armando called, his voice joyous.

'Ten thousand apiece,' Raval called, his voice full of shaky confidence.

Teed heard the heavy tramp of slow footsteps coming up the stairs from the second floor. Armando gave Teed a puzzled look. Teed moved over to the railing and looked down, careful not to expose himself to the men who waited down the hall to catch them as they moved off the stairs.

Mark Carboy was plodding slowly up the stairs. He was muttering to himself and he held the fantastic revolver in his hand.

He glanced up at Teed with no recognition and continued up, his heavy breath wheezing with the effort of the climb.

'Who's coming?' Raval called nervously.

Carboy reached the hallway, turned to the right, toward Raval and Stratter. He lifted the revolver and fired. The explosion in the confined place seemed to lift them into the air. Teed was deafened. There was a hard, persistent ringing in his ears. Carboy sat down like a fat baby, spraddle-legged. Teed saw two little puffs of dust leap out from the front of his dark overcoat. He held the gun with the muzzle resting against the floor. His face was bland, unalarmed. He bit his lip and tried to lift the gun. He got it up a few inches, but the muzzle sagged back. He grasped it with both hands. As he tried to lift again, a round black dot appeared on his forehead, above his left eye. He leaned slowly forward, both hands still on the gun. The muzzle slid along the rug.

Raval vaulted the body, dived down the stairs. He managed to keep his feet. They heard his hand slap hard against the wall at the landing and then he was gone. Teed had been too frozen to fire at him.

Armando moved cautiously into the hall. He turned back at once. 'Scratch one Stratter, Teed. Christ, what a cannon!' He pulled it out of Carboy's dead hands. 'There's still three in it.'

They went down the stairs. Castle Ann seemed to be deserted. A starter began to whine. The motor churned over and over and over, but didn't catch. The sound stopped. A wide-eyed girl bounced into the hall, stared at them, darted back into her room and slammed the door.

Teed's leg had begun to grow weaker. He began to limp as he went down the stairs. A lot of blood had been lost. The world seemed to rush toward him for a moment of sparkling, incredible clarity, and then recede again into remoteness.

Armando sat down suddenly on the stairs and coughed. Bright blood spilled over his lips, splatted on the bare wood.

'I think it touched a lung,' he gasped. 'My breathing has been sounding funny.' Again he touched the dark haft of the knife with his fingertips, almost tenderly.

Teed left him behind. He walked across the lobby. The starter of the car whined again, fruitlessly. A car door slammed and there were hurrying footsteps on the gravel. Raval, full in the lights from the bar window, came trotting around the corner of the building on Teed's right. He no longer looked bold and confident and overpowering. He was a frightened man who ran with hunched shoulders, underlip pulled grotesquely down.

In the distance the high wild sweet song of a siren drifted across the night fields. Trees had begun to stand out against a hard metal greyness in the east.

Raval tried to stop too quickly, and fell to his hands and knees, dark metal skittering out of his hand, whispering along the gravel. He pounced toward the gun. He was a tiny figure, a thousand miles away. He was a bug under a thick grey lens that was full of wavering imperfections. The gun in Teed's hand recoiled twice and Teed did not hear the shots. A giant reached down from the grey sky and swung a flabby finger against Teed's shoulder. It spun him around and dropped him on his face, gravel smashing his lips and grinding against his teeth. After a long time he got up onto his hands and knees. The night was full of a screaming that he could not identify. The corner of the building was at the other end of the world. He crawled there. He shut his eyes and rammed his head into the side of the building. He sat back stupidly, corrected the course.

She lay against the side of the building where she had been roughly tumbled off the hood of the big car. The impact had dished it deeply, sprung the front of the hood up. She lay on her side, the sleazy yellow satin housecoat balled in the small of her back.

He grunted busily to himself as he spread the house coat out. He rolled her onto it and pulled it around her. The zipper started at the bottom hem. It was hard to get it started. He clucked and muttered and finally the small metal teeth meshed. It made a purring sound as he pulled it up to her throat, covering the whiteness that was not smashed, not bleeding — just subtly wrong, obscurely out of proportion.

He wormed around on his haunches until his back was against the thick front bumper, against the bug-dotted sparkle of the chrome, and then he eased her head into his lap.

When the spotlights centered on him, he squinted into them, lips drawn back in an uncomprehending, death-head grin. His tongue fumbled loosely and heavily with the words as they bent over him. 'Top floor. Girl.'

In some bright place, much later, Leighton's cadaverous face slid down from a blazing sky of a dozen suns and loomed over him. The thin lips wormed and the words all leaned wetly against each other so that there was no meaning. 'WasRavalshot? Washehurt?'

'Later, later, later,' a shiny voice said.

'Was Raval hurt?'

'Don't know,' Teed said. 'Don't know. Don't know.' He stopped saying it, but it went on and on in his mind until the words had no meaning. Where Leighton's face had been there was a tunnel. It slid down and sucked against his lips. In the tunnel the unspoken words whined emptily off the sides, echoing into forever: 'Don't know. Don't Know. DON'T KNOW!'

And then, running down toward him, down the slant of tunnel toward him, she came running, running, gladness in her throat and in her eyes a joyousness too great to be born.

He stood arms outstretched for her to run into his arms. And she ran against him and he shuddered because she was formed of cold stone and she wore Barbara's face on her broken body.

15

The nurse had a face the color of wet wash and hair like copper wire. She was slat-bodied and smelled of talcum.

She rolled the chair close to the bed and beamed at him. 'Today we can spend some time on the sun porch. Isn't that wonderful?'

He looked at her. 'Just too gay.'

The smile slid off her face. 'Now turn and get your hands on the arm of the chair. I'll steady it. Lower yourself into it, please.'

He did as she told him. He came down into the chair with more force than he had expected.

'Would you like to take something along to read?' she asked.

'No.'

She came around the chair and stared at him. Her blue eyes were severe. 'Mr Morrow, a large part of rapid recovery is the patient's attitude. I think you ought to let those people come and see you. I'm sure it would cheer you up.'

'Would it?'

'See how sour you talk to me?'

He took a deep breath. 'Look, Miss

Mission. Sooner or later I'll have visitors. At the moment I don't want to see them. I don't want to read the papers. I don't want to do anything except listen to the world go around and the grass grow.'

'It was bad, wasn't it? That poor girl and the way . . . '

'And I don't want to talk about it. I've told you that before.'

'Mr Seward is very insistent. He comes twice a day, Mr Morrow.'

'Tell him to kindly go to hell, Miss Mission. Now wheel the wheel chair.'

Her shoulders slumped. Her uniform made a starchy rustle as she shrugged. She pushed the chair out through the room door and down to the elevator. The elevator took them to the top floor. The sun porch was having a busy morning. All conversation stopped as he came in and he saw the avidity of their eyes. The victim of a real honest-to-Gawd gun battle. Sure. He's the one. Two slugs in him. Come in here with about a pint of blood left. They give him plasma all the way to town in the ambulance. Found him rocking that dead girl and talking to her.

'Over there in the corner,' Teed said.

She left him. 'I'll be back in an hour. If you want anything, that nurse over there will get it for you.'

Her heels made dull sounds on the composition floor as she walked out, distributing her professional smile on all and sundry. The silence lasted for just a few more moments and then the others started talking in low tones. Teed grasped the wheel rails and turned the chair so that his face was in the sun, his back to the room.

He could not stop thinking of his life as a chart on a wall in the back of his mind. The level line had reached placidly to that Sunday, three weeks ago, when he had awakened in the camp, had heard the sound of Felice's shower. Then the line had begun to waver. It had fallen off for the next week, and then it had stopped. Now there was no line at all. Not depression. Just a nothingness. Somehow life had changed from a pleasant game where you're all right if you keep your guard up to a mess where your guard didn't help a bit. And once you knew that, none of the old rules were any good any more.

The only visitors had been Leighton and the police stenographer. It had been impossible to keep them out. Later the stenographer had come back with the stack of copies of his statement, and he had scrawled his name in the indicated places.

'They got Raval,' the stenographer said.

'That's nice,' Teed said tonelessly.

'Picked him up at Tampa International Airport. He had a ticket to Mexico City. He'll be inside until he falls over his beard.'

'That's nice,' Teed said. The stenographer gave him a curious stare and left.

In an hour the redheaded nurse came back. In the elevator going down she said, 'A Miss Dennison is waiting to see you, Mr Morrow.'

'Tell her to . . . no, I'll see her.'

Marcia came into the room. She wore black. She sat primly, quietly, on the chair beside the bed. 'Teed, I want to know what your plans are.' He nodded.

'Daddy is quitting. He can't stay here, now. The University wants him back. Everyone is willing for you to take his place. If you don't want it, he wants to look for another man.'

'I haven't decided, Marcia.'

'Could you decide right now? It would help him. He . . . needs help. He's a defeated man, Teed.'

'Aren't we all.'

She looked at him with the level eyes, her father's eyes. 'Did you love her so very much, Teed?'

'That's one of the things I've been thinking about. I didn't love her at all in the way you mean. Not as a woman. I . . . keep thinking of what I should have done that would have prevented it.'

'You couldn't do anything.'

'It was my fault that the whole thing started in that way. I gave them the handle to use on Jake.'

'They would have found some other way. Don't torture yourself by blaming yourself. Jake . . . wouldn't want you to.'

He smiled at her. 'Powell used to try to get you and me together. I was the son-in-law elect.'

She stood up, pulling her black gloves nervously through her fingers. 'That sort of thing is done. I'll stay with him. I shan't marry anyone.'

'That's what you've been all along, isn't it, Marcia? A cool-eyed martyr looking for a stake to be tied to.'

She looked down. 'Don't spoil it, Teed. Please. When they made me, they . . . left something out. Jake had it all. I used to resent her. Almost hate her at times. That's my guilt, Teed.'

'Tell Powell I'll take over just as soon as I can get out of here.'

'Mr Trim is co-operating. The grand jury will be set to go. Daddy has new information and we ought to get a return of indictments on fourteen men in the city government. Then he'll leave it in your hands.'

'In a year I'll have it running the way it

should. Then I'll find somebody who wants to stay in one place and turn it over to them.'

She stood by the bed. 'Get well soon, Teed.'

'I'm too tough to kill,' he said. She took his hand, then bent over and kissed him on the forehead. After her footsteps were gone he still felt the cool impression of her lips. Viking woman. She of the sturdy thighs, of pelvic width for the bearing of children, of breasts meant to sweeten and flow. This would be a waste, just as the death of Jake was a waste. The years would dry and harden her, and the juices of youth would parch in the wind of barren years. In a way it was a little death, and he wondered if, in part, it were her penance for Jake's death.

The lunch tray came. His appetite was getting better. Even the drab hospital food, attractive in colour rather than taste, was welcome.

The nurse came to take the tray. 'Is Barbara Heddon still in the hospital?'

The nurse started so violently that the empty dishes rattled. 'Uh . . . yes.'

'Why did you jump?'

'I just happened to be thinking about her when you asked me that. That's all. I was wondering about it. You never asked about

her before, and she never asked about you.
That's all. It seemed funny. So I was thinking
about it.'

'Has she had visitors?'

'Her people, from Baltimore. That's all.
Nobody local.'

'Was Armando Rogale discharged?'

'After four days. A fat woman came and
took him home with her. Mrs Ferma or
something.'

'Can I see Barbara Heddon?'

'I'll ask the doctor. She's not supposed to
move.'

'Let me know.'

Late in the afternoon Barbara's doctor
came in and pulled up a chair. 'You want to
talk to the Heddon girl, eh?'

'If it's all right. How is she?'

'Apathetic. And that's good. I like that. I
don't want that face wrinkling up with a lot
of emotions. Not until healing is further
advanced.'

'Will she be . . . badly scarred?'

'She thinks so. I don't. The left eye was
ticklish. Thought at first it would have to go.
But I did a hemstitching job on those eye
muscles. Proud of it. Going to write it up.
Like sewing a pair of wings back onto a
housefly.'

'How about the scars?'

'It was a nice sharp edge. Clean slashes. Right side already OK. But there was tissue loss on the left side. Her left arm is straight up over her head now. I'm telling you this in a way you can understand it. Cut a flap from the underside of her left arm, gave it a half turn and used it as a patch on the left cheek. Left it fastened to the left arm until the graft is far enough along. Then we'll cut it free and do some trimming. A face like that, it's a pleasure to do cosmetic surgery. Damn good bones. Be a pretty woman when she's sixty. I won't say you won't be able to see hairline scars in a bright light when she isn't wearing make-up. I let her folks see her. Had to chase them out when she started getting a little upset. No smiling and no frowning for that young lady until I'm certain those healing muscles won't tear under the strain. That's why you can't see her. Not for ten days, Morrow.'

'Tell her I'm coming to see her.'

'I told her that a week ago. She said for you to stay away from her.'

The doctor stood up. 'Be good,' he said. He trudged out, a big weary man on an endless treadmill.

★ ★ ★

Teed was discharged at the end of the week. Five days later the doctor phoned him at City Hall. 'Morrow? Come see the Heddon girl at two this afternoon.'

'Has she changed her mind about seeing me?'

'No. But now I want her stirred up. I want her to rant and rave and storm around, using all the facial expressions in the book. Got to start getting back muscle tone, or she'll end up with a dead pan. All slack. She won't tear now. Healing fine. But apathetic. Don't like that. Go give her a hard time. Nurse expecting you.'

Teed put the transcript of his grand-jury testimony in the locked file. Miss Anderson gave him a sallow nod as he said he would be gone most of the afternoon.

He checked out with Powell Dennison. The heart was gone out of the man. Now he was merely an old man who worked mirthlessly, doggedly, and without satisfaction at the things he knew best.

Teed parked in the hospital lot at ten of two. The receptionist told him the room number, told him to go right up. A pretty nurse stood waiting in the hall. She held her finger to her lips, opened the door to let him in, closed it soundlessly behind him.

Barbara lay with the bed cranked up to

bring her almost to an erect sitting position. Her knees were elevated and she was turning the pages of a magazine. A bandage covered the left side of her face, from hairline to chin. Her nose, right eye, and the right half of her mouth were uncovered. A smaller bandage was taped to her right cheek.

She gave him a startled look and reached for the signal button. He reached it before she did, took it to the length of the cord and put it on the window sill.

She had not spoken. He pulled a chair over, sat down, took her hand. She tried to pull it away, but he held it tightly. She let it go lax. Her hand had the damp coolness of nervousness.

'They're going to make you beautiful again, Barbara.'

'Is that important?' Her voice was listless.

'It will be nice. I'm going to spend a long time looking at you. But even if they couldn't, it wouldn't matter too much.'

She looked at him gravely. 'Don't be a sentimental fool. Run while you can.'

'I've spent a lot of years running, Barbara. I'm tired of running. Now I've found something that helps me make sense out of living. A . . . sort of talisman.'

'A good-luck charm,' she said, her voice bitter, distorted by the constriction of the bandage across the left side of her mouth.

'Be rough. Be bitter and nasty and pretend you're hard as brass hinges, baby. It won't do you any good.'

'You want to look at a face like this?'

'When I get tired of looking, I'll turn out the lights.'

A tear spilled over the lower lid of her eye, channelled down by her nose to her lip. She caught it with the tip of her tongue. 'All cats are grey in the dark.'

'Suppose I love you, though. Suppose I spend more time thinking than ever before in my life, and I find out I love you. What then?'

'I chase you away, Teed. Because I don't want you to keep remembering what I was, torturing yourself with it. And you'll do that. After a while it would come between us and you'd look at me and think of it and hate me. I don't want that.'

'I've given that considerable thought, Barbara. I've tried to be logical. It bothers me. It will always bother me. I admit that. I know why it will bother me. Because in the formative years they give you books about virgin princesses. Romantic books. They condition you to a double standard where a man is a man and a woman is not really human. So it is hard to remember, always, that a woman is human, not some kind of a damn sweet-smelling toy on a store shelf. I've done too much sleeping around. It isn't good. It dulls your taste.'

'That isn't the same.'

'I make a ledger in my mind. On one side I put this business of remembering what you were doing when I met you. On the other side I put all the things you have come to mean to me. And that leaves me right where I started. Needing you.'

She rolled her head restlessly from side to side, as though she were seeking escape. 'Don't, Teed. Please don't talk like that to me. Please go away.'

'In eight months to a year this job will be over for me, and it will be turned over to local people. I know you're going back to Baltimore. Here's all I want. Go back. You're mending on the outside. Mend on the inside, too. We'll write letters to each other. When this job is over, I'll come to you. We'll talk. That's all I want. A chance to show you that nothing will change in a year. Or twenty years.'

'Why tie yourself up to a tramp?' she pleaded.

'Tramp? A man is one thing one day and something happens and he is suddenly somebody else. Maybe you have to be honest with yourself. Too honest. You have to say to yourself, 'I was a tramp'. O.K. Say that. But don't say, 'I am a tramp', because you know that would be a lie, and I know it too.'

She looked up at the ceiling. 'There is another way I would be unfair to you, Teed, if I didn't send you away. I . . . can't have children.'

'That was a nice try, Barbara, but you talked too much to Anna Fermi. I had dinner there with Armando and Anna last night. We talked about you. Anna happened to mention that you told her that you could have children.'

'Damn you, damn you, damn you!'

'They are my friends. I suddenly discover that maybe I never had better friends. We talked about you. I told them how I feel about you. We talked over whether or not I could forget that other business. Then Anna did a smart thing. She asked me if I would forgive you. I stared at her and I asked her what the hell for. Then she gave me that grin of hers and said that I had given the right answer and so she thought it would work out for us.'

'Leave me alone.'

'See? I'm pushing you out of a little death you've made for yourself back into life. You're reluctant. I checked with another person too.'

'Maybe a letter to Emily Post would help.'

'I checked with Albert. Albert said that in his work he has to understand pigeons, but he'll be damned if he can understand women. He told me to tell you that, such as it is, we have his blessing.'

And on her face was the twisted mixture of tears and laughter, bitterness and joy. 'Albert was . . . always dopey.'

'He told me how stubborn you were when you were a little kid. He said I should use force if necessary. I said I didn't want to use force. I said I would make a dramatic appeal. I told him that I would tell you that if you insisted on having nothing to do with me, life would cease to have any meaning at all to me.'

'Teed, don't . . . '

'Albert said that sounded too corny and too dramatic. I told him it was the truth, and I couldn't help it if it sounded that way. Albert said, O.K., then, for me to try it, but it certainly wasn't going to work on the Barbara he remembered.'

She turned toward him. Her unbandaged eye was shining, bright, tear-filled. 'That shows you how much Albert knows about women.'

His voice was husky. 'Albert better stick to his pigeons.'

Her hand tightened in his. 'I shouldn't let you . . .'

'You're not agreeing to a thing. Only to letting me come to see you when this job is done and we're both a year older.'

'Don't ever let me hate myself for wanting to say yes to you, Teed.'

'When we start tossing crockery, we'll bring Albert in as referee. Darling, laugh again. I love your *love*!'

'I'll laugh for you. I'll laugh in the night. Not for funny. Joy laughter. Love laughter. Laughter for being alive.'

He kissed the right corner of her mouth. He tasted the salt on his lips as he straightened up.

'Tomorrow we'll talk some more.'

'Yes, Teed.'

'There's a lot to say to you, Barbara.'

'I know.'

'Tomorrow we'll talk about how in that other life, we were two different people, neither of them as sound as you and I. The old life didn't happen to us.'

She frowned. 'That's odd! I can almost believe you.'

'One day you will.'

He walked down the soundproofed hall, and down the stairs, and out into the fat wet flakes of a late November snow. The flakes melted as they touched his face. He walked to his car, feeling that at last he had stepped from the sidelines into the midst of life. There could be no more detachment. Only involvement. You did the very best you could with everything you could reach. And never stopped reaching, or trying. And this, at last, made life a satisfying thing — a thing at which you were given one chance — and learned to enjoy the knowledge that one chance was all there was.

THE END

We do hope that you have enjoyed reading this large print book.

Did you know that all of our titles are available for purchase?

We publish a wide range of high quality large print books including:
Romances, Mysteries, Classics
General Fiction
Non Fiction and Westerns

Special interest titles available in large print are:
The Little Oxford Dictionary
Music Book
Song Book
Hymn Book
Service Book

Also available from us courtesy of Oxford University Press:
Young Readers' Dictionary
(large print edition)
Young Readers' Thesaurus
(large print edition)

For further information or a free brochure, please contact us at:
Ulverscroft Large Print Books Ltd.,
The Green, Bradgate Road, Anstey,
Leicester, LE7 7FU, England.
Tel: (00 44) **0116 236 4325**
Fax: (00 44) **0116 234 0205**